Guitar Notes

Mary Amato

EGMONT
USA
New York

Hear all the songs from the book, sing with the karaoke tracks, and learn how to write your own songs on the *Guitar Notes* website, www.thrumsociety.com.

EGMONT
We bring stories to life

First published by Egmont USA, 2012
443 Park Avenue South, Suite 806
New York, NY 10016

1 3 5 7 9 8 6 4 2

www.egmontusa.com

www.maryamato.com

Book design: ARLENE SCHLEIFER GOLDBERG
Illustrations and design elements: MAX AMATO

Library of Congress Cataloging-in-Publication Data
Amato, Mary.
Guitar notes / Mary Amato.
p. cm.
Summary: Tripp, who plays guitar only for himself, and Lyla, a cellist whose talent has already made her famous but not happy, form an unlikely friendship when they are forced to share a practice room at their high school.
ISBN 978-1-60684-124-2 (hardcover) ~ ISBN 978-1-60684-300-0 (e-book)
[1. Interpersonal relations~Fiction. 2. Musicians~Fiction. 3. Guitar~Fiction. 4. Cello~Fiction. 5. High schools~Fiction. 6. Schools~Fiction. 7. Single-parent families~Fiction.] I. Title.
PZ7.A49165Gui 2012
[Fic]~dc23
2011038115

Printed in the United States of America

In memory of my dad, Jack Koepke, whose hearty rendition of "On the Road to Mandalay" was the beloved soundtrack of my childhood car rides; for Mr. James McCauley, my eighth-grade English teacher in Libertyville, IL, whose lesson on song lyrics as poetry made my soul thrum; and for all the singers with whom I have sung, most especially the earliest ones: my sisters—Cathy, Nancy, and Suzanne—and my high school friends-in-harmony, Jane Donndelinger Victor and Mary Donndelinger Neuberger.

1. Wear the white belt.
2. Pick up your guitar.
3. Tune.
4. Play.

—from *Zen Guitar*
   by Philip Toshio Sudo

SEPTEMBER 2. TUESDAY.

Tripp Broody's Room; 7:33 a.m.

. . . BUMPER-TO-BUMPER DUE TO AN ACCIDENT ON THE LEFT SHOULDER. RESCUE CREWS ARE ON THE SCENE. UP-TO-THE-MINUTE TRAFFIC BROUGHT TO YOU BY MONTGOMERY AUTOPARTS . . .

The clock-radio alarm drills into Tripp Broody's ears, and his eyelids open. After three slow blinks, he realizes what he is seeing three feet from his bed: a note taped to the metal stand where his guitar should be.

He sits up, pushes his long, messy hair out of his eyes, and reads it.

1

Dear Tripp,

I know you're going to be mad at me, but you didn't keep up your end of the bargain. You didn't do your summer reading or math packet. You didn't do anything but lock yourself in this room and play the guitar. It's like you're addicted to it. It's unhealthy and isolating. You are capable of getting straight A's. You can have your guitar back if you have all A's at the end of the semester and if you at least attempt to be more social. Don't bring a sour face to school. Nobody likes that. Talk to people this year, okay? It won't kill you.

Love, Mom

P.S. You have brought this on yourself. I really believe that you're going to thank me for this in the long run.

It takes a moment for the reality to sink in. His room is hot and small, the air conditioner wheezing out a pathetically small stream of cold air molecules.

He wants to scream, but he keeps his mouth closed. She must have planned it all out, he thinks, to take his guitar on the night before school begins so that there would be no time to discuss it. She is a thief and a coward.

2

After pulling on shorts and a T-shirt, he walks into the kitchen, takes her bag of ground coffee out of the cupboard, and pours the coffee down the garbage disposal. Then he walks over to a potted aloe plant, spoons dirt into the coffee bag, apologizes to the plant, neatly refolds the top of the bag, and puts it back in the cupboard.

Finely ground French Roast dirt.

Take that.

Lyla Marks's Room; 7:34 a.m.

Lyla Marks is lying on her bed, staring at the ceiling, fully dressed, her frizzy dark hair fanning on the white pillow like a fern. Her heart is beating abnormally loudly. She puts her hand over it. *Calm down.*

Her phone buzzes. She knows without looking at the little screen that it's Annie. She doesn't want to hear her friend's voice right now, because she knows that it'll make her heart beat even faster. But she answers.

"What are you wearing?" Annie asks.

"Tangerine top. Blue skirt," Lyla says.

"And the shoes that I picked out?" Annie asks.

"Yeah. I'm lying on my bed. I feel like a corpse."

"That's sick. Stop talking like that. You're freaking me out," Annie says. "We're picking you up in five minutes. Be ready."

3

Lyla slips her phone into the pocket of her jean skirt. Her black cello case is on its side in the middle of her bedroom floor. She imagines opening the window and pushing the case out, imagines it splitting open when it hits the ground, and the cello splintering into pieces.

"Lyla!" her dad calls.

She picks up her cello and walks out the door.

Her dad is at the bottom of the stairs, looking at his phone. "Dr. Prevski just e-mailed. She said yes to adding an extra fifteen minutes to your lessons so you can work on the Coles audition piece!"

Lyla's heart starts pounding again. "That's great," she says, and busies herself by checking what's in her backpack.

When Annie's car pulls up, Lyla's dad picks up her cello and follows her out. "Play the Bruch piece," he says. "Just the second part. That'll show Mr. Jacoby your range."

"Got it, Dad," she says, and smiles.

"Have a great first day, sweetie!" He puts the cello in the back and says hi to Annie's mom as Lyla gets into the car.

"Lyla, you look adorable," Mrs. Win says.

"Just absolutely adorable," Annie says, and laughs.

"Thank you," Lyla says to Mrs. Win.

"You both look adorable," Lyla's dad says as he closes the back of the car.

"We don't want to look adorable," Annie says. "We want to look sophisticated."

As Mrs. Win is about to pull out, Lyla's dad knocks on the window.

Lyla looks out.

"Where's your head? Put your seat belt on," he says through the window.

"Sorry," she says, and buckles up.

"Ready?" Mrs. Win asks.

"Yeah," Lyla lies.

ROCKLAND SCHOOL; 8:05 A.M.

Tripp wants to turn around and make a run for it. Too many students are streaming through the school doors at the same time, yelling and laughing. As soon as he's inside, a girl next to him screams at another down the hall. "Beanie, you look totally cute!"

Beanie screams back, "Casey, I missed you all summer!"

Tripp turns to the girl called Beanie, who he doesn't know at all, and asks, "Why did you just lie?"

"What?" The girl gives him a look.

"From the sound of your voice, it's obvious you're lying," he explains.

"From the sound of your voice, it's obvious you're an idiot." The girl runs ahead.

Who wants to hear the truth? Nobody. Well, he talked

to someone today. He can tell his mom that. He adjusts his headphones and turns up his music.

Mr. Handlon, the vice principal, is standing outside the main office. "Welcome back, Alex. Nice to see you, girls! Tripp Broody, headphones away or they're mine."

"I promise to put them away when I get to class," Tripp argues.

"Put them away now or they're mine. You know the rules."

Reluctantly, he puts away his music and is pushed forward by the crowd. The shouts and clatter, along with the smell of fresh paint, make him dizzy. He pulls his schedule out of his pocket—Intro to Tech in Room T113—and heads toward the T hallway.

"Hi, Mrs. Sykes!" a girl next to him calls out. "How was your summer?"

It's oval-faced Annie Win, with her friend Lyla Marks, famous at his school. Perfect at being perfect. They are passing him, walking fast, carrying their instruments, happy to see their teachers, happy to be back. "Do your brains sing chipper songs inside your chipper heads all day?" he asks them.

Annie throws him a foul look and pulls Lyla to the bulletin board in front of the music room. Tripp notices what they're reading: MUSIC PRACTICE ROOM SIGN-UP.

"Patricia Kent already has her name up here!" Annie exclaims.

He stands behind them and peers around Lyla's hair to read:

MUSIC PRACTICE ROOMS
AVAILABLE FOR USE
DURING LUNCH PERIOD.
SIGN UP BELOW
FOR THIS SEMESTER.
THE SCHEDULE WILL
BE POSTED ON SEPTEMBER 8,
AND ROOMS WILL OPEN
SEPTEMBER 15.

While Annie writes her and Lyla's names on the first two lines, Tripp scans the bulletin board and sees another notice: BAND/ORCHESTRA STUDENTS NEEDING TO SIGN OUT A SCHOOL INSTRUMENT, PLEASE CONTACT MR. JACOBY ASAP.

"Let's go," Annie says, and they head into the orchestra room.

Tripp gets out a pen. Under Lyla's name he writes:

> Tripp Broody (not a band or orchestra person) would like a practice room (if the school has a guitar to borrow).

He begins to leave and then stops and adds:

This is not a joke. This is a matter of survival.

ROCKLAND HALLWAY; 3:15 P.M.

As soon as the final bell rings, Tripp heads to his locker, and his phone buzzes.

Mom calling.

"I'm not talking to you, Mom."

"How was school?"

"I said I'm not talking to you."

"I spoke with your algebra teacher at lunch," his mom says. "She'll only take off two points if you turn in your summer packet at the end of this week."

"I spoke with God today. He'll only take off two points if you confess your sins and return my guitar."

"Very funny. Look, I know it was probably a shock—"

"I can't survive without my guitar."

"See. It's like you're addicted to it. This will be good for you to take a break and focus on—"

"I can't do it."

"I warned you so many times this summer. I know it's a drastic step, but I don't know what else—"

"Is it in the attic?"

"It's not in the house, so don't go tearing it apart. Oh, that reminds me. The guy is supposed to be there at four to do the termite eradication thing. Take him to the base-ment and show him that wooden rafter they're eating through. The one I showed you. He's supposed to spray it with poison and put in some kind of traps or some-thing."

"You do realize that you are a termite," he says. "You are eating through my soul."

"Very funny."

"I am an empty shell. I am going to crumble."

"Go home and fill yourself up with math problems. I'm going to check them tonight. Bye."

Tripp closes his phone, slips it into his back pocket, and makes his way down the noisy hallway. When he walks outside, the bright beauty of the day stabs him.

SEPTEMBER 3. WEDNESDAY.

Tripp's Room; 7:01 a.m.

"Tripp!" His mom's voice bites the room. She's standing in his doorway, holding up the bag of dirt. "Where's my coffee?"

He turns to face the wall and pulls up the sheet. The Termite has arrived.

She marches over. "This is completely immature. Where did you put it?"

"Maybe it went to visit my guitar."

"You better not have thrown it out."

He turns to look at her. "You sound so tense, Mom. It's like you're addicted to it."

She gives him a look. "If you think that by messing

10

with my coffee, you're going to get your guitar back, you're dead wrong. I can always buy more coffee, Tripp. And I'll be sure to take it out of your bank account."

The Termite storms out. He sticks out his tongue at the door as it slams. Is he immature? Yes. If maturity means you can grow up and take away the one and only thing that gives meaning to your son's life, then why would anyone strive for maturity?

SEPTEMBER 4. THURSDAY.

ORCHESTRA ROOM; 8:56 A.M.

With Mr. Jacoby on the podium, the Advanced Orchestra is playing through a new piece — a new teacher, a new year — and Lyla is waiting for the entrance of the cellos. Her index finger is just above the spot on the A string where her first note will be, but a dark little fantasy is flickering through her mind like a ten-second horror film: when she presses down on the string, a bomb that has been rigged inside the cello will explode.

She knows it's just her imagination, but her palms are sweating and her heart is racing. As a new metronome amplifies an annoyingly loud, incessant clack, the violin bows leap in perfect unison, and all the cellos to her right pounce on their opening measure, but Lyla's hands do not move.

Her heart is beating too loudly. Maybe the muscles around her heart are squeezing too tightly? Is that possible? *Calm down*, she tells herself. *Jump in on the next measure.*

"Measure sixty-four," the boy next to her whispers, his voice purring with the satisfaction that for once Lyla Marks has lost her place.

She begins to play, and the cello does not explode. Her left hand fingers the pattern of notes, and her right hand holds the bow, but it feels as if her hands belong to someone else and she is merely attached to them.

"More energy!" Mr. Jacoby calls over the rising sound.

After the piece is over and the teacher is giving comments, Annie Win turns around, scrunching her eyebrows and pumping her shoulders up and down to imitate him. Lyla forces a smile.

When class is done, she is relieved to put her cello away.

"Jacoby is a joke. Everything we did is too easy," Annie whispers. "And Jessica needs to brush her teeth. I should tell her."

"You can't just say that," Lyla whispers back.

"Maybe I'll put mouthwash on her music stand." Annie makes another face and pulls Lyla out the door. "Jessica said that Ms. Collivet wants to start a French club and she'll give anybody who joins an automatic A."

"Annie," Lyla interrupts. "I think I might . . . do you think it's possible for someone our age to have a heart attack?"

Annie laughs. "I saw a show on TV where this really young guy had a heart attack and he had a disgusting nipple ring and when the doctor put the defillibrator, or whatever it's called, on his chest, the electricity hit the metal ring and electrocuted the doctor!" Annie starts laughing. "So the moral of that story is, don't try to save anybody who has body piercings."

"Who has body piercings?" Kenneth Chan is on their heels.

"Lyla does," Annie says.

"I do not!"

Annie laughs, and then as soon as Kenneth passes by, she whispers, "He likes you, but his nose is too big."

Lyla hears her own heart beating even above the noise in the hall. She shifts her books, pressing them against her chest to dull the sound. "Annie, has your heart ever been so loud that you could hear it without a stethoscope or anything? "

"No." Annie stops. "Is your heart being weird?"

"Sort of."

"That's what the first week of school does." Annie shrugs it off. "It gives you a heart attack. Hey, remember that time in fifth grade when you swore to me that you could hear your bones grow? For, like, six weeks I tried to listen to my bones." She laughs and leads the way into the English room, which is noticeably hot and stuffy.

Sweat prickles on Lyla's forehead. *Stay calm.* She has to get through school.

Annie turns and whispers, "If you die of a heart attack and leave me alone this year, you know what I'll do?"

"What?" Lyla asks.

"I'll kill you." Annie laughs.

SEPTEMBER 8. MONDAY.

ROCKLAND HALLWAY; 8:19 A.M.

As Tripp is walking to class, he notices the music teacher posting a sign on the music bulletin board.

PRACTICE ROOM SCHEDULE 11:26–12:10
ROOM A: PATRICIA KENT EVEN DAYS;
ANNIE WIN ODD DAYS.
ROOM B: LYLA MARKS EVEN DAYS;
TRIPP BROODY ODD DAYS.

"Thank you. Thank you!" Tripp says.
Mr. Jacoby turns and looks at him. "Tripp?"
Tripp nods. "You have just saved my life."

"Well, I don't know about that. I found one guitar in storage. This program really focuses on band and orchestra."

"What kind of guitar is it?"

"Acoustic, steel strings, but the strings are shot." Mr. Jacoby frowns. "You'll have to provide your own."

"I don't mind, as long as I can play. Can I take it home?"

He shakes his head. "No. You're not in the music program here. Technically, the instruments can be checked out only by students in the program. We'll keep it in Room B. By the way, two of these girls are serious musicians and would like to practice every da—"

"I'm a serious musician, too."

"I wasn't implying that you aren't. If you decide that you don't want to use the room, just let me know right away so that I can reassign it. The rules are posted in the rooms: One person per room; the computers in each room are to be used only for music—no video games or surfing the web; clean up after yourself."

"Got it. Thank you."

Mr. Jacoby heads into the orchestra room, and Tripp continues on his way to class. He has been allotted precisely forty-four minutes of joy every other day, beginning next Monday. Something inside him bubbles up and he leaps into the air.

"What was that supposed to be?" one girl behind him asks another.

"I don't know. Who does that?"

He laughs. "I do."

ABEL PHOTO STUDIO; 3:58 P.M.

The studio is large and white. In the back, a gray cloth is draped on the wall and floor. Lights are set up on either side of the cloth, facing in.

The photographer shows Lyla into a dressing room. While she is changing into her performance dress, she hears her dad taking her mom's cello out of the case. He starts explaining to the photographer that he wants to include one photo in her Coles application and wants to send the other to the local newspaper with a note about her upcoming Kennedy Center audition.

Her phone buzzes. When she sees that it's Annie calling, her heart pounds even harder.

"Where are you?" Annie asks. "I looked for you after school."

"At the dentist, remember?" Lyla whispers. "I told you about it yesterday."

"Are you done? Ask your dad to drop you off here."

"I'm in the waiting room. I haven't even gotten in yet."

"Call me as soon as you're done."

"Okay," Lyla agrees. She tucks the phone into her backpack and hangs it on a hook. Then she takes a deep breath and walks out.

"Great dress," the photographer says. "Beautiful choice." He asks her to stand on the cloth, and her dad brings the cello to her.

"This is going to be very easy," the photographer says, stepping behind the tripod. "Piece of cake. All you have to do is smile."

Lyla forces a smile.

Click.

SEPTEMBER 15. MONDAY.

Rockland School; 11:23 a.m.

Tripp isn't sure where the practice rooms are located. As he turns down the hallway toward the orchestra room, Annie Win passes him, walking in the same direction. Black hair as straight and silky as a doll's, falling all the way down to the middle of her back. Crisp yellow capris. Matching yellow sandals. Ankles that have never been dirty. He imagines that instead of showering, someone merely brushes her off with a feather duster.

She opens the orchestra room door, and when he follows her in, she looks back and scowls. "What are you doing here? You aren't in orchestra or band." Her eyebrows are high and pointed rather than rounded in the middle. Her voice is like a rapid-fire laser gun.

"I'm installing new carpeting," he says.

"You are so strange," she says.

"Yeah. We're putting it on the walls to dampen the sound. People over in art have been complaining about the violins."

She makes a face, turns, and gets her violin case from the storage room. He notices the dead-end corridor in the back of the room and, guessing that the practice rooms are there, heads toward it.

She is at his heels. "Seriously. Why are you here?"

"I signed up for a practice room."

"I saw your name on the sign-up list, but I thought it was a joke. It's not fair for you to get a room," she says. "Mr. Jacoby told me and Lyla that we can't have rooms every day because somebody else wanted one, too. I thought it was an orchestra person."

He stops and she bumps into him.

"Why isn't it fair?" he asks.

"These rooms are for *music*."

"Yeah, well, you band and orchestra people are not the only musicians in the world."

She stalks into Room A with a slam of the door.

Perfect girls think they own the world.

Tripp walks into Room B and immediately wants to shout with joy. It's small, but perfect. Blank white walls, a workstation with a computer, an electronic keyboard, and cool recording devices. Way better than he expected.

Go, Rockland School. And there's the guitar—waiting just for him.

Eagerly, he closes the door, moves the bench to the side, lays the battered case on the floor, and opens it. The sight of the guitar cracks his face into a smile. He runs his fingertips along two big scratches on the front. Four of the six strings are gone; the two that remain are gummy and old. It's beat-up, but it doesn't matter. It's a guitar.

Tripp pulls a packet of strings out of his backpack and gets to work. The minute the guitar is in his hands, his body is pumped with energy. One by one, he changes the strings, and then he uses the keyboard at the workstation to find the right pitch for each string, ignoring the muffled scales of Annie's violin next door.

Sitting on the floor, he pulls his pick out of his back pocket and strums. He rests his right hand on the body of the guitar, feeling the vibration of the wood, listening to the sound, and something inside him comes alive. It's as if there are six strings inside him, tuned to the same pitches, and when the guitar is strummed, it causes his strings to ring out, too.

Well, well, well, he thinks, *the Termite will not be able to devour my entire soul.*

SEPTEMBER 16. TUESDAY.

ROCKLAND HALLWAY; 11:24 A.M.

"Let's get out of this oven." Annie pulls Lyla out of the English room.

"It's an even day," Lyla says. "I get the practice room today."

"Hey, when you see Patricia What's-Her-Name, ask her to switch days with me, then we can both practice on even days."

"What?"

"That lowly French horn player. She has Room A on even days. Ask her to take it on odd days, and I can take even days with you and we can have the same lunch schedule. We only have morning classes together. It's not fair."

The responsibilities of the week are scrolling through Lyla's mind in a continual loop: the new cello piece for the Coles audition, the U.S. history project, French quiz, the club Annie wants them to join, reading for English, algebra problems, science, Saturday's Metz Youth Orchestra rehearsal, the Kennedy Center audition . . . her heart beating faster and louder as the loop goes on.

It's like the story she read last night for English class. "The Tell-Tale Heart" by Edgar Allan Poe. One man murders another and stuffs the body under the floorboards. When the police come, the murderer believes they can hear the beating heart of the victim and so he confesses, but it's really his own heart beating in his ears. No! Her life is not like that at all. She didn't murder anyone. What does she have to feel guilty about? Why is she thinking of that story?

Stay calm, she tells herself, *and your heart will slow down.*

"Ask her!" Annie repeats.

"Okay," Lyla says.

Annie scowls as they thread their way through the crowd. "You sound like that's a bad idea."

"I said okay."

"Your voice was weird."

"It was not, Annie. Why wouldn't I want us to have the same lunch schedule?"

Annie nods toward a girl down the hall. "Look at Marisse's calf muscles. She probably exercises in her sleep. She thinks every guy is always drooling over her. I hate her. She's in all my afternoon classes."

They reach the B hallway and say good-bye. Lyla continues past the media center by herself. *Breathe in. Breathe out.*

A trio of girls pass by and say hi. Lyla smiles and waves, catching a glimpse of herself in the glass of the trophy case: She is Lyla Marks. Everyone loves her. She is on her way to the music room to practice during lunch because that's what she does. She is a cellist. This defines her, separates her from others. She is the first-chair cellist.

Breathe in, she tells herself. *Breathe out.*

After she takes her cello into Practice Room B and closes the door, she gets it out of the case, lays it on the floor, and stares at it for several minutes. She glances up at the ceiling, checking for hidden cameras that she knows are not there. Lately, she's been feeling as if she's being watched, even when she knows she's not.

Breathe in, she tells herself. *Breathe out.*

Slowly, her heartbeat regulates, the tightness in her chest loosens.

The little room helps. The fact that no one is watching her.

Trash on the music stand catches her eye. The odd-day guy must have left it. Tripp Broody, the guy who criticized her and Annie for being "chipper." She glances up to check that the rules are still posted there from last year. NUMBER THREE: DISPOSE OF ALL TRASH IN HALLWAY TRASH

CAN. It makes her mad when people don't follow the basic rules.

She breathes and looks at the guitar case. It's scuffed, one lock unhinged, the handle attached with duct tape — the odd guy's domain. Even the case looks like him. In contrast, her cello is unblemished and polished, lying on its side on the floor, like a whale that has washed up on the shore. She should pick it up, resuscitate it with her bow. Instead, she calls up her MP3 files of cello music on the computer and plays them so anyone who passes by the room will think she's practicing. After she is finished eating her lunch, she will practice, she tells herself. She eats her lunch in tiny, tiny bites.

SEPTEMBER 17. WEDNESDAY.

PRACTICE ROOM B; 11:23 A.M.

An odd day, the only kind of day that counts. Tripp barely hangs on to consciousness through Intro to Tech and Spanish, but then he walks through the orchestra room and opens the door of Practice Room B. It's the energy of the room he loves, this quiet peace that is just waiting to be filled with sound.

Hello, little room.

The room likes him. He can tell. He sets his lunch on the workstation and opens the guitar case. A piece of white paper, folded neatly, is tucked between the strings. An unexpected development.

Dear Odd Day Musician,

We are sharing this room. Please remove your trash from the music stand when you are done. Thanks.

—The Even Day Musician

Lyla Marks has left him a note. He flips the paper over and writes his reply.

Dear Ms. Even Day,

Thank you so much for the little note you left in the guitar case.

The napkin that I left on the music stand was not trash. I wrote a chord progression on it. Did you throw it away in your quest for a perfect spotless world?

Most Sincerely,

Mr. Odd Day

P.S. Please do not leave negative Even Day vibes all over the room. They will soak into this guitar, which will ruin it. Please clean up after yourself.

He folds it and leaves it on the music stand.

SEPTEMBER 18. THURSDAY.

Practice Room B; 11:22 a.m.

Lyla sees the note right away, and as she reads it, her face grows hot.

She was right, and he knows it. She hates people who try to make other people feel stupid just because they choose to follow basic rules of politeness.

She calls up the cello music on the computer and pushes up the volume. She tells herself that she will, in fact, practice the cello today, but only after she writes Mr. Odd her reply.

SEPTEMBER 19. FRIDAY.

PRACTICE ROOM B; 11:23 A.M.

As Tripp opens the door to Room B, he hears his name and turns around.

Annie Win, violin case in hand, hops into place. "Lyla has your room on even days. If you trade with her, you would get even days, and Lyla and I could have odd days together."

"No," he says.

"Why not?"

"I like odd days."

"They're exactly the same. What difference does it make?"

Tripp shrugs. "Odd days are better than even days." As

he closes the door, she huffs. Poor perfect girls can't have what they want. Too bad. He has Intro to Tech and science on odd days; he needs the little room to survive.

Opening the guitar case, he smiles to see a second note, folded and tucked like the first.

Dear Mr. Odd,
   Forgive me for mistaking your chord progression for trash, but you also left a candy wrapper and a crumpled napkin on the music stand. I thought I had chipper vibes, not negative ones. Well, you can make fun of me and my "vibes" for being bothered by trash, but at least I am considerate of others. Clean up after yourself and you won't have to read any more of my "little notes."
   —The Even Day Musician

The note is like the pickle in his sandwich: a tangy crunch to make the bread of his morning and afternoon classes less boring. After he plays, he'll have fun writing a reply.

The guitar practically jumps into his arms. He loves this moment, when his fingers are ready to find something: a chord, a pleasing phrase, something worth repeating, something worth following.

SEPTEMBER 21. SUNDAY.

TRIPP'S ROOM; 6:11 P.M.

Josh and his friends sitting on somebody's couch. Josh and his friends knee-deep in snow. Josh shooting a free throw in a crowded school gym. Tripp is staring at the photos on Josh's efriends page. He hardly recognizes his old friend. Since when did he play basketball? He looks happy in Schenectady, wherever that is.

He clicks SEND A MESSAGE. Then he stares at the blank box. After a minute, he clicks X to close the site. He has nothing to write about.

On the wall behind his desk is a photo he took of his dad sitting on a log in front of their tent. It's dark, but the light from the fire shows his wide smile and lights up all the goofy wind chimes they hung in the trees—the spoons and spatulas, the old hubcap and the bathtub faucet handles, the kiddie xylophone parts they had found by the side of the road. He can smell the smoky warmth of the fire, the scent of the loblolly pines, and the musty smell of the tent.

If they were there right now, they'd be taking one last look at the lake before they had to come back. His dad always said that: "Let's take one last look at the lake."

Tripp forces his gaze back to the computer. What he needs to do is learn a new riff, a new trick. He searches YouTube until he finds a good guitar tutorial and tries to follow along with the guy, but without a guitar, he just gets more frustrated. After a minute, he stands up and yells at the top of his lungs: "I NEED A GUITAR."

He hears the heavy roll of his mom's car pulling up the driveway, flicks off his laptop, closes it, and crawls into bed with the assigned short story for his English class. Edgar Allan Poe. "The Tell-Tale Heart."

The main character murders a guy. Tripp is hooked. The story is gothic and full of orphaned phrases that he plans to adopt:

. . . hearkening to the death watches

. . . all in vain

. . . Villains!

Over the wheeze of the air conditioner, he hears his mother and their neighbor Susan talking in the driveway.

"The Slater Creek Parkway Cleanup Committee needs

a chairperson, Terry; you'd be perfect," Susan was saying. "All you have to do is sign up on the Slater site."

"It's a great cause, Susan, but I don't really have the time—"

Susan. Susan. Susan. Do you really want a termite like Terry Broody on your cleanup committee? Tripp tunes them out and reads on. . . . In the story, the guy's heart is beating so loud, he thinks it is his victim's. A bizarre horror story. This kind of homework he doesn't mind.

When he is done, he stares up at the ceiling, trying to block out the sound track of his mother's entrance into the house, the click of her heels in the kitchen.

"Tripp . . . you home?"

He puts his hand on his chest to see if he can feel the beating of his heart. He cannot. Has he died in bed? He closes his eyes and tries to hear his heart pumping blood through his veins. He gets up and looks at himself in the mirror.

Boom Boom. Boom Boom. He thumps his chest with his palm. Boom Boom. Boom Boom. Over the boom-boom beat, he is dying to play a searing guitar solo. But alas, it is all in vain, all in vain, because Death—in the form of his mother—has eaten away the very thing he loves. Villain! Thy name is Termite!

As if on cue, his mother enters. She sees the book on his bed. "Edgar Allan Poe! Ooh. I remember those stories! Which one are you reading?"

He knows what she is doing. She is trying to engage him

34

in a cheerful discussion about literature so that he will forget her cruel kidnapping of his guitar. He looks at her in the mirror. "I'm sure you know the assignment, Mom. It's posted on Edline. And, yes, I finished reading it."

"Well . . . I was just stopping in because I learned something interesting today. Did you know that your school offers peer tutoring during lunch hours?"

"No. No. No. No. No."

"It would make such sense. You hate lunch anyway. You've told me that."

He can't tell her about the practice room. She would pull the plug for sure.

"I think I should sign you up for it," she says. "It's a *peer*. You might hit it off. Make a new frien—"

"No. No. No. No. No—"

"I don't understand that word." She turns and leaves. "I'm signing you up."

Villain!

He paces for a while, and then he opens his laptop and calls up the Slater Community Association website. After he finds the page for the Slater Creek Parkway Cleanup Committee, he clicks the sign-up button.

I would like to be chairperson for this committee: yes
Name: Terry Broody
E-mail address: tbroody@broodyrc.com
Comment: I'm so excited to become a part of this great cause.
Submit: Yes

How wonderful of the Termite to sign up for such an important community-building event. Maybe she'll even make some new friends!

SEPTEMBER 22. MONDAY.

PRACTICE ROOM B; 11:26 A.M.

Tripp Broody has left no trash in the room, not a single piece of paper, and Lyla realizes that she was hoping for another acerbic note.

Good, she tells herself. *I shouldn't waste my time with him.* She sits on the bench and eats half a tuna fish sandwich and an apple and tells herself that, as soon as she is done, she will get out her cello. But after a few bites, she sets down her lunch and opens the guitar case. A note, folded, is tucked between the strings.

Dear Ms. Even,

You are well known for being absolutely perfect. Perfect grades. Perfect behavior. Perfect posture. Perfect attendance. Perfect class president. Perfect cello playing. Perfect best friend who plays perfect violin. I heard you sneeze once. Even that was perfect.

My question is, why choose to get all worked up about a trifle? How long did it take you to throw away my wastepaper products? 3 seconds? 3.5 seconds? Now, how much negative energy have you wasted being mad at me because of it? What is the point? Why couldn't the candy wrapper on the music stand inspire you to write a song? That would be a positive way to handle it. Perhaps I'll write one called "The Even Day Vibes."

-Mr. Odd

Lyla reads it twice, mashes it into a ball, marches into the hallway, and throws it into the trash can. She comes back in and paces, four steps from wall to wall, her heart racing. Then she pulls out her notebook.

Dear Mr. Odd,

Thank you for enlightening me on the subject of why I am so petty and negative and shallow. Here are my apple core and the crusts of my tuna fish sandwich. I truly hope these objects inspire you.

—Ms. Even

She drops her sandwich crusts and apple core on the music stand like little bombs. She feels wicked, better somehow.

She paces. One, two, three, four. One, two, three, four.

Through the walls, she can hear the muted sound of Patricia Kent's French horn. She should go next door and ask if she'd be willing to switch days with Annie, but instead, she gets out the guitar.

Two big scratches run down the front. The ends of the strings at the top are messy, coiled. He didn't even bother to wipe off the dust.

She sits down on the bench with it. There's a worn black strap, but she isn't sure if she should put it on. How different to hold an instrument in her arms, like a big baby, instead of resting it against her body. She lays the fingers of her right hand on the strings. No bow.

Pluck. Pluck. Pluck. Pluck. Pluck. Pluck.

Funny. She was expecting to hear the notes C, G, D, A—the four strings of the cello—plus two more. It takes her a moment to figure out the pitches of the six strings: E, A, D, G, B, E.

She studies the neck. Is it fretted chromatically? Each fret a half note? Can she play a scale?

She experiments until she finds the E major scale. Plays it up and down. Then the E minor. Up and down. Each note rings out in the little room.

The strings are new. She can tell. New strings always have a bright sound.

As her fingers move through the scale, she tells herself that everything will be all right. She is Lyla Marks. She is just playing this guitar for a moment because it feels good to play it, and then she will pick up her cello because she is a cellist, and she is an A student, and she is Annie Win's best friend, and her heart is beating normally, and everything is perfectly fine.

When the period is over, she puts the guitar away reluctantly. She tucks her note for Mr. Odd in between the strings, closes the case, and sets it back in the corner.

"Ah, Lyla." Mr. Jacoby startles her. "Just the person I was looking for."

Guilt shoots through her like adrenaline, and she spins around. Did he hear her playing the guitar? Did he see the apple core and the sandwich crusts on the music stand?

He holds the door for her and she picks up her cello. He follows her to the storage room, where she puts away her instrument. "You did very well on the Bach this morning." He laughs. "That's an understatement. I've never heard anything like it. International Culture Day assembly is October third, and Mr. Steig is hoping that a music department student will perform a short opening piece, and I'd love you to do something." As they walk out of the storage room, he opens the file he is holding and pulls out the sheet music. "I was thinking of Allegro Appassionato by Saint-Saëns. I bet you know it. Or would you like to do another piece?"

She imagines telling him that she'd rather not play, imagines Mr. Jacoby disappearing in a puff of smoke.

He looks at her anxiously. She hears herself say yes she knows the Saint-Saëns piece and yes she'd love to play and thank you for asking, and his face jumps into a smile as he hands her the music.

"And it goes without saying that I'm hoping you'll want to participate in the juried competitions this year," he says. "The first one is in November, and I was thinking of this piece." He pulls another piece of music out of the file and hands it to her. "Take a look at it and tell me what you think. I'd be happy to meet with you anytime after school or during lunch. I'm so excited to be working with you!"

She glances down at the music. A multitude of black notes race ferociously across the page, setting off ripples of panic that she feels in her chest.

"Better hurry or you'll be late for your next class," he calls out.

She stuffs the music into her folder. *This is a good thing,* she tells herself as she hurries down the hall.

SEPTEMBER 23. TUESDAY.

PRACTICE ROOM B; 11:23 A.M.

It is an odd day, and Tripp Broody is happy to be back in the little room.

Immediately, he smells something fishy and sour and then finds the source: crusts of what must've been a tuna sandwich and a withering apple core on the music stand. He opens the guitar case, reads her note, and laughs out loud. Leaving the trash was probably the worst thing Ms. Even Day has ever done in her A-plus perfectly obedient life. How fun it would be to call Mr. Jacoby in and show him the trash that the perfect Ms. Lyla Marks left behind, but he'd rather keep the exchange of notes going.

He puts her note in his pocket and, as he picks up the

guitar, he notices that the black strap is half around one side of the guitar instead of underneath the body. As he positions the guitar on his lap, he feels like one of the three bears: Someone has been sitting in my chair; someone has been eating my porridge; someone has been playing my guitar.

He will write a new note. But first he wants to play.

"Ode to Apple Cores and Sandwich Crusts," he thinks to himself, and he begins.

ROCKLAND HALLWAY; 3:14 P.M.

Lyla is at her locker, trying to decide what she needs to bring home, when Annie catches up with her.

"Guess who I overheard in the bathroom," Annie says.

Lyla's brain is spinning over details. English and science homework will be due on Thursday; algebra and French are due tomorrow. As she puts the books she needs into her backpack, she says, "Give me a clue."

"They're in your section in orchestra."

"Brittany?"

"Yep. And that other girl. The new one who always braids her hair."

"Julia."

Annie nods, eyes flashing. "They said Jacoby gave you a solo for next week's assembly."

Lyla's heart pounds. "It's true."

"Why didn't you tell me?"

"I don't know. I—"

Annie punches her arm. "Because you thought I'd hate you, which I do! You should've heard them. 'Lyla gets everything.' They really hate you." She laughs.

"Oh. Thanks. Great news." She closes her locker and pulls her cell phone out of her purse.

"You are envied, Lyla. That's a good thing. If you didn't have any talent or you were stupid, then nobody would envy you." Annie pulls her down the hall.

"I'm not sure I want to be envied. Do you think we have a kind of reputation . . . like of being . . . perfect?"

"Of course!" Annie says.

"But maybe being perfect isn't such a great thing."

"What is wrong with you? Being perfect is what everybody wants to be."

Lyla's chest tightens. "I don't think everybody wants to be perfect."

"Those are just the poor peasants. Speaking of peasants, did you ask Patricia What's-Her-Name to switch days with me?"

"She said no," Lyla lies.

"NO? Why?"

Lyla shrugs. "Some schedule thing. It was complicated."

"If Lyla Marks asked me to switch days, I'd say yes. Oooh. I hate her."

"You don't even know her. She felt bad about it." Lyla's cell phone rings.

44

"Let me guess," Annie says. "How was school today, sweetie?" she asks in perfect imitation of Lyla's dad.

Lyla has to laugh. "Hi, Dad," she answers. ". . . yes . . ."

"Remind him that we're staying for the Sweet Tooth Club," Annie adds. "And say good-bye, sweetie."

Lyla turns her back to her and finishes the conversation. As soon as she puts her phone away, Annie pulls her down the hallway.

"We can't be late."

Lyla winces. "I don't know if I even want to be in Sweet Tooth."

"We need Sweet Tooth."

"Who says?"

Annie stops. "The Coles Conservatory of Music. I already put it on my Coles application, didn't you? My mom said they look at stuff like clubs and community service. And Sweet Tooth is brilliant because it's both a club and a community service project. 'We donate all our sales to charity.' Did you seal up your envelope yet?"

"I don't think so."

"Double-check. Put it in. When are you going to actually mail yours?"

"I don't know."

"Let's go on Saturday to the post office. I'll get my mom to drive us and we can mail them at exactly the same time. It'll be good luck. Just think, next year at this time, we'll be at Coles and—"

"You keep saying that. We haven't even applied. We

don't know if we'll even be invited to audition."

"My mom said the fact that we did the conservatory camp this summer gives us an edge, plus we've been stars in Metz Youth Orchestra for the past gazillion years and we aced all the state competitions last year. And now we'll have Sweet Tooth to show we are community-minded. Oh, I already put that lunchtime thing where we tutor little people with small brains to show we're smart—"

"It might not be possible to do all that," Lyla says.

"Shut up!"

"We can't do the lunchtime tutor thing together anyway because of the practice room thing."

"We do the tutor thing on the days we're not in the practice room. Patricia What's-Her-Name deserves to rot. If she traded, then we could do everything on the same days." Annie leans in. "Well, put it down on your application and sign up for it anyway. I already did. We have to do everything we can."

Lyla groans, and Annie gives her a look. "All right, Lyla. We can quit Sweet Tooth after we get in to Coles."

"First of all, we might not get in to Coles. Second of all, we can't just quit Sweet Tooth whenever we want!"

Annie rolls her eyes. "What do you think, they put us in handcuffs? YOU MUST BAKE FOR GOOD CAUSES!"

Lyla laughs. "They might."

"Okay, then we won't quit." Annie steers Lyla down the next hallway. "We'll just take it over and become

Cupcake Dictators and eat all the baked goods and become even more well rounded. Très, très round! That's what we did with *The Quill* last year."

"We did not."

"We did, too. We totally took it over. We made it thirty-two pages instead of sixteen. Color instead of black and white. We got to use the lounge instead of the media center, and basically, Mr. Jordan just said yes to whatever we wanted." Annie pulls Lyla into a classroom and then whispers: "Marisse and Casey are here. Smile."

Lyla forces the corners of her mouth up.

SEPTEMBER 24. WEDNESDAY.

PRACTICE ROOM B; 11:46 A.M.

Dear Ms. Even,
   You have been playing this guitar,
haven't you?
   —Mr. Odd

Dear Mr. Odd,
   I do not play the guitar. I play the cello.
   —Ms. Even

SEPTEMBER 25. THURSDAY.

PRACTICE ROOM B; 11:37 A.M.

Dear Ms. Even,
   The guitar is crushed. It wants to be played. Thankfully, it has me.
   —Mr. Odd

SEPTEMBER 27. SATURDAY.

THE BROODYS' CAR; 11:03 A.M.

Tripp's mom eases the car out of the driveway and puts the air conditioner on full blast. "I bet Lorinda is nervous," she says. "Take those things out of your ears, Tripp. It's rude."

"Lorinda is an unpleasant stick insect who deserves any unhappiness that might come her way," Tripp says flatly, tucking his earbuds into his pocket.

"Don't say that! She's your cousin."

"Lorinda tied me to a chair, put a sock in my mouth, and locked me in Aunt Gertrude's attic when I was four."

"She did not."

"I was traumatized, Mom. You have chosen to block

50

this and the numerous other acts of Lorinda's evil out of your system. She pinned me down another time and tried to literally replace my pupils with watermelon seeds. I don't care if she is related to us. The girl is insane."

They drive for a while and then his mom pulls into a store parking lot and gets out.

"What are you doing?" Tripp asks.

"Picking up the doves." The door slams. Tripp watches her try to run in her black patent leather heels. She comes out two minutes later carrying a wicker basket shaped like a heart, and she hands it to Tripp. "It's too hot for September," she says. "I'm going to die in this dress."

Through the slats in the basket, Tripp can see a black eye. He lifts the lid slightly. "They're pigeons," he says. "They look drugged."

"Doves." She buckles up and pulls out. "After the wedding ceremony, I'm supposed to open the cage and release the birds. It's like a symbol of their love."

"The basket stinks." Tripp puts it in the backseat. "Somebody sprayed it with fake-flower perfume."

"Better that than bird droppings," his mom says.

When they arrive, the church is packed. A trio of musicians is playing a slow, plodding melody. Piano, flute, classical guitar. The groom and four groomsmen are standing on the right, looking hot and uncomfortable. Tripp is dying to grab the guitar and run.

The parents of the groom walk down the aisle, and then the mother of the bride comes, his mom's older

51

sister, who always wears the same bitter expression.

Tripp nudges his mom to look at the priest, who is asleep in a chair next to the lectern. "The music bored him to death," Tripp whispers.

His mother's eyes widen. "He better wake up."

Tripp starts to laugh and she shushes him.

The priest wakes up, the wedding begins, and the musicians play another coma-inducing tune.

To stay awake, Tripp slips cracker crumbs that he has found in his pocket into the birds' basket. One of the doves pecks up the crumbs as soon as they drop. The other dove doesn't move. They haven't made a sound. What kind of bird remains silent when imprisoned? he wonders. Shouldn't they be screaming their heads off?

After the ceremony, they all gather in the stifling heat on the steps outside the church. The limousine pulls up, which is the cue for the birds.

Tripp's mom holds up the basket and lifts the lid.

Nothing happens.

She hoists the basket with a quick small motion and one of the doves flies up.

A few people clap, but everyone is still waiting.

She tilts the basket and hoists it up harder. The second bird falls out and lands on the concrete with a dull thud.

Another silence. In one quick move, the groom's father kicks the corpse into the bushes.

No one says a word.

Lorinda gives an exasperated look and pulls on the groom's arm. "Let's just go."

As they get into the limousine, a few people begin to clap and everyone joins in.

"Congratulations!" someone calls out.

Tripp's mom looks like she's going to be the next one to hit the pavement.

"It's not your fault," he whispers. "You did a great job."

She throws him a doubtful glance.

"Really, Mom. They gave you a very elderly bird."

She smiles.

His hugely generous heart has leapt free of the cage of anger to bestow compassion on the lowly Termite in her time of need. He can only hope she will remember this.

POST OFFICE; 2:22 P.M.

Annie gives her application package to the clerk, takes the large padded envelope from Lyla's hand, and sets it on the counter. "They're both going to the same place."

"Anything fragile, liquid, or perishable in these?" the clerk asks.

"Just our fates," Annie says to him, and he laughs.

"An application and a DVD," Annie's mom says. "The girls are applying for a special music school. Priority mail, please."

Annie grins at Lyla. "This is sooooooo exciting."

He stamps PRIORITY MAIL on each envelope.

"Do you have a good-luck stamp you can put on it?" Annie asks.

The clerk smiles again and shakes his head. Annie's mom pays, and, as he tosses their envelopes in a shipping bin, Lyla feels her stomach drop.

"Good luck," he says. "Next in line."

"Now all we have to do is wait," Annie says. "The suspense is going to literally kill me. I'm going to die."

"Yeah," Lyla says. "The headlines are going to read: Two girls got accepted into the Coles Conservatory of Music but died of suspense before finding out." As soon as it is out of her mouth, she knows she's just going through the motions. *I don't want to go to Coles.* She says the truth to herself as they walk out.

"Enough of this!" Annie's mom says. "We're going to celebrate. It was a project just getting those applications together and out the door. What'll it be? Ice cream or frappuccinos?"

SEPTEMBER 29. MONDAY.

PRACTICE ROOM B; 11:37 A.M.

Dear Ms. Even,

   I have superhuman ear cilia to pick up vibes, and your even-day vibes have been all over this guitar. So on Friday I snuck in and stood next to the practice room door and hearkened. At first I thought it was all in vain because there was cello music, but I pressed my ear to the crack in the door and lo and behold what did I hear? The beat-beating of the telltale heart? The tiny hooves of reindeer? No. I heard this guitar. Scales.

Liar liar strings on fire, you are playing this guitar. The cello music on the computer is your cover. You have that on so nobody hears you playing the guitar.

So you're a closet guitar player, Lyla Marks. I have two theories. Number One, you secretly want to be a Rock Goddess, but you are worried that people will make fun of you because you are quite the opposite of a Rock Goddess. (Rock Goddesses use picks, play power chords, and wail.) Or Number Two, you read in a book that you can play the cello even more perfectly than you already do if you strengthen your fingers by playing another instrument and so you're just doing this so you can play Bach more beatifically and add mozzarella to your Mozart, which will give you an edge so you become a cello star. Which one is it?

    —Mr. Odd Day

56

SEPTEMBER 30. TUESDAY.

Practice Room B; 11:48 a.m.

Dear Mr. Odd,

How pleasant to think of you stalking me. What business of yours is it if I am playing the guitar? You do not own it.

Okay. I am playing it. Are you happy? And I don't have to tell you why. Please do not tell anybody. It's not because I'm embarrassed or anything. It's just that there's a lot of pressure on me. I am playing a solo in front of the entire school on Friday, and I have a Kennedy Center audition on Saturday. I really should be practicing.

—Ms. Even

P.S. Did you put the strings on right? They are messed up at the top. You should ask Mr. Jacoby if it's okay to fix the scratches on the front. There's this wood filler stuff you can get in a tube. Look it up on the Internet.

OCTOBER 1. WEDNESDAY.

Practice Room B; 11:39 a.m.

Dear Ms. Even,

This is the guitar writing. Your secret love for me is safe with Mr. Odd. He does not engage in gossip.

I am somewhat hurt by the casual remarks about "fixing" my scratches. Does everything have to look perfect to be worthy? If you would only hearken! I have a great sound—warm and golden—especially with the new strings that the talented and charming Mr. Odd put on, and, indeed, he put them on right.

Some people clip the ends of the strings off close to the tuning peg and some people make "loops" at the top.

Perhaps Mr. Odd <u>likes</u> the mess at the top. A reminder that life is messy.

—The Guitar

P.S. Scales are boring. If you're going to play, <u>play</u>.

OCTOBER 2. THURSDAY.

Practice Room B; 11:36 a.m.

Dear Mr. Odd,
    You are indeed odd.
—Ms. Even

OCTOBER 3. FRIDAY.

ROCKLAND SCHOOL AUDITORIUM; 9:04 A.M.

". . . and now to play Allegro Appassionato by Camille Saint-Saëns . . . here is Lyla Marks." Mr. Handlon nods at Lyla, who is waiting in the wings.

Applause.

Lyla picks up her cello and walks to the black metal folding chair that is waiting for her onstage. Her dad is standing off to the side with his video camera on a tripod.

Her heart is pounding. Tripp's words are in her head: If you're going to play . . . *play.* As she sits, she feels the eyes of the audience on her face. Someone calls out something, and a few students laugh.

She imagines that she is not Lyla. She is a fake one, with arms made of metal, the one programmed to perform today. A computer chip in her brain will fire the neurons that will make her fingers move. The real Lyla is still waiting in the wings.

She lifts her bow and begins.

SPANISH CLASS; 10:53 A.M.

Greetings, Ms. Even,

I'm in Spanish class right now and I'm bored out of my finely constructed skull. To stay awake, I could either chew on the spiral binding of my notebook thus inducing metal poisoning or I could ask you this question about the International Culture thing. Please don't take this the wrong way.

I was there first period, sitting in the back, not paying any attention at first because assemblies are always a joke, and then Mr. Handlon introduced you.

Two guys in front of me snicker. "What's she gonna play?" one of them says.

"'The Fart of the Bumblebees' by Mozart," the other guy says, and they both laugh.

"Play some Lady Gaga," the first guy calls out.

Just so you know that wasn't me.

I don't know if you saw it, but a paper airplane flew from the back to the middle of the auditorium, and some people laughed. You looked up then like they were laughing at you, but they weren't. People laugh at flying paper.

You sat down and started to play like it didn't really matter if anybody heard you or not.

Everybody got quiet, the two guys in front of me even. One of them says, "She must practice fifteen hours a day." Awe. Respect.

But that's not why I'm writing.

Here's why I'm writing. I looked at your face really carefully, and I think you're faking it. You make your face look like you're into your music and everything, but I don't think your emotions were real. You weren't really thrumming.

Am I right? I'm not criticizing you. I'm just fascinated by people faking things, *so I guess I just want to know, does playing the cello make you happy?*

—Mr. Odd

P.S. I hope you don't think I'm stalking you or anything because I'm not, but I saw you at your locker yesterday, so I'm thinking, why not slip this note into your locker instead of the guitar case because that way you'll get it today instead of waiting until Monday. Not that it makes any difference really.

Tripp finishes writing the P.S. and folds the note. The three vents near the top of Lyla's locker look like the gills of a fish, like the locker is alive and needs to exhale. Tripp feeds the folded end of his note into the top slit and hears the *phump* of it landing in the creature's stomach. Too late to get it back.

ROCKLAND HALLWAY; 11:26 A.M.

Lyla opens her locker to get her lunch. A small tent of folded paper is sitting on her locker floor, writing scrawled on both sides.

As a locker ahead of her slams and a girl laughs, Lyla opens the note and reads.

It's like the words have been written with fire and she's breathing the flames straight into her lungs.

A freckle-faced girl taps her. "You were so good this morning!" the girl gushes, her arm linked in the arm of her friend.

"Unbelievably good," the friend says.

Lyla feels herself smile and hears herself say thanks. The girls walk on, and Lyla turns to the letter again, holding her breath.

I just want to know, does playing the cello make you happy?

Annie's squeal startles her. She's coming her way. Quickly, Lyla folds the letter and puts it into the back pocket of her jeans.

"We have twenty-seven hours until the Kennedy Center audition!" Annie is breathless. "I'm soooo lucky today is an odd day. I can practice. Come with me and we'll kick Tripp Broody out. Of all days, today you should have the practice room."

Lyla can't think.

Annie pulls her down the hall. "I really want you to sleep over tonight, Lyla. If you don't, I'm going to be neurotic about the audition all night. Ask your dad again."

They walk down the hall. "He said no. He wants us to be well rested. And he thinks we should drive separately."

"He doesn't trust my mom's driving skills."

Lyla laughs. They stop at the intersection where they will go their separate ways.

"Oh!" Annie grabs Lyla's arm. "Curt said Jacoby put up the sign-up sheet for the talent show. What time slot do you want to go for?"

"Annie, can we talk about this later? I'm feeling so overloaded." Lyla stops breathing for a moment. She and Annie don't really talk, do they? Annie just bulldozes over everything Lyla says. She presses her pocket, crinkling the stiffness of the paper.

I just want to know, does playing the cello make you happy?

"Fine, but we're signing up on Monday before the good slots get taken."

Lyla stops. "Hey, Annie. Do you have Tripp Broody in any classes?"

"No. Why?"

Lyla hesitates. "He stuck this note in my locker."

Annie's voice pierces Lyla's eardrum. "WHAT? He's an alien. What does it say?" She lowers her voice to a whisper and comes closer. "Does he like you? You cannot go out with Tripp Broody. I'm going to pick a boyfriend for you, and you're going to pick one for me, and we're going to all go out together."

"I'm not going out with him. It was just a comment. Forget it."

"What did he say?"

"It was just about the assembly. It was nothing. See you la—"

Annie grabs her. "You can't just say it was about the assembly. I need details."

"He said I was good, but that I looked like I was faking it."

"What is that even supposed to mean? He is sooooooo bizarro. Beanie said he made some rude comment to her on the first day. Did I tell you how rude he was when I asked him to switch? Do not listen to him!"

"I won't. Promise you won't say anything to him."

"I have no interest in saying anything to him," Annie says, heading toward the music hallway and calling back, "We're talking about this later!"

"It's not a big deal, Annie!" Frustrated, Lyla turns and walks toward the cafeteria.

As soon as she arrives at her usual table, all her friends tell her how great she was this morning. She smiles and says thank you and tries to embrace the routine. She is Lyla Marks the cellist. This is the way it has always been. She needs to stop thinking odd thoughts about the cello exploding and needs to stop being annoyed by everyone complimenting her and needs to stop panicking when it's time to practice or play. Mr. Odd is making it worse. It isn't fair of him to stare at her face during a performance. Who said he's allowed to put her under a microscope? Before the lunch period ends, she escapes to the bathroom. There, she takes out her notebook and writes a reply to Mr. Odd. She'll figure out where his locker is and slip it in.

Dear Mr. Odd,
    I received your letter about me faking it. What a nice thing to tell someone before a big audition.
    Before I start, I will ask the judges not to expect much because I will be playing without a soul and not thrumming, whatever that means. Oh, and I'll make sure to return all the first-place trophies that I have received, since I must have won them by faking it.
    —Ms. Even

OCTOBER 4. SATURDAY.

KENNEDY CENTER STUDIO L105; 2:30 P.M.

Violinists are warming up in a separate studio, which is one consolation; a solid wall separates Lyla from Annie's nervous buzzing. Lyla's father is bad enough. He is sitting too close, drumming his fingers on his thighs and eyeing the cellists who are packing up and the two others who are still waiting to audition. "Wouldn't you feel better if you played through your scales?" he asks for the second time.

She is holding her mother's cello, trying to hide the dread on her face. Before she can answer, a woman with a clipboard walks in and calls her name.

70

Her dad stands up. Lyla nods and stands and gingerly picks up the instrument.

"Be careful going through the door!" her dad whispers, and then adds, "You'll do great."

"Beautiful instrument," the woman says. Then she stops. "Lyla Marks." Recognition flushes over her face. "You're Gwendolyn Marks's daughter!"

Her dad beams.

The woman's eyes get watery. "I heard her with the National Symphony right upstairs," she whispers to them both. "I think I'll stand by the door and eavesdrop on this one!"

Lyla's dad wishes her good luck again, and Lyla follows the woman across the hall.

Six judges are sitting in wooden chairs behind one long table. In the center of the room, an empty chair waits for her.

Lyla turns to fit the cello through the doorway.

"Good luck," the woman whispers.

Lyla sits, trying to imagine what the judges are seeing in her face. Can they tell that she doesn't want to be here? *I will make a mistake*, she says to herself, *and they will reject me, and it will be over.* She feels her mother's ghost crouched inside the cello, peering at her.

She lifts her bow and plays, her fingers marching solemnly up and down the neck. She doesn't make a single mistake.

OCTOBER 6. MONDAY.

PRACTICE ROOM B; 11:36 A.M.

Dear Ms. Even,

You took it the wrong way. I mean that you're faking your enthusiasm, not your skill. You're copying and repeating something that somebody wrote a long time ago, but you're not into it. You're like a machine. Just tell me if I'm right. I was at a wedding last week, and the musicians were like that. Really good, but not really playing.

Every time I pick up my guitar, I _play._ I don't copy and repeat music that somebody else thinks is good. I play what's inside me. That's what I mean by thrumming. When the vibrations of the music make your soul vibrate, you feel the thrum. It's like you're perfectly in tune with the song, as if you are the music and the music is you. It's the only thing I do that feels right. I know Mr. Jacoby thinks I'm not a serious musician because I'm not in band or orchestra, but I think a serious musician is somebody who really thrums.

   —Odd

OCTOBER 7. TUESDAY.

PRACTICE ROOM B; 11:37 A.M.

Dear Odd,

Thank you once again, O Wise One, for the enlightenment. I think a serious musician shares his or her music. What is the point of thrumming if you never do it outside of your little room?

I think it's beautiful and profound that Saint-Saëns wrote something down and I can read the music and play it on a stage and add beauty to the world. I think it's my responsibility to add beauty to the world. Perhaps this is why I also dispose of my own trash.

By the way, I came to the music room

yesterday and stood outside the practice room, listening—or should I say, hearkening—to you play. I don't have superhuman ear cilia like you do. I have regular ears, but I could still hear you. Do you ever play a real song or do you always play in that formless way, one guitar solo after another like a string of random phrases? Don't take this the wrong way. You were probably playing your heart out, but how satisfying is it to play that way? Are you happy?

—E

OCTOBER 8. WEDNESDAY.

PRACTICE ROOM B; 11:42 A.M.

Dear Even,

Thank you so much for your encouraging comments regarding my music. I didn't realize that my songs aren't real. Do songs have to adhere to a form to be real? Do you always know where you are going when you walk? I enjoy peregrinating in a random fashion. Sometimes I enjoy peregrinating and eating a pomegranate at the same time. While I'm doing that, my phrases might meander, but what can I do?

As for your last question, I don't need the Kennedy Center's seal of approval. I am perfectly happy to peregrinate all over the map. Alone.
Sincerely,
The Formless Peregrinating Meanderer (Otherwise known as Odd)

Lyla reads the note several times, and then her phone buzzes with a text message from her dad.

Dad/congrats! You made the KC audition! Just got the call! Couldn't wait to tell you!

Her heart sinks.

Lyla/did Annie make it?
Dad/don't know. I'm so proud of you.
Lyla/thanks dad. got to go. talk later.

She puts away her phone and paces back and forth in the little room. It's a big deal, the Kennedy Center program. She should be excited.

She gets out her cello music , sets it on the music stand, and stares at it. Then she rereads Tripp's note. Finally, she calls up the cello music on the computer, turns up the volume, and picks up the guitar.

OCTOBER 9. THURSDAY.

PRACTICE ROOM B; 11:27 A.M.

No note from Ms. Even. Tripp is disappointed and wonders if he went too far, if he offended her. She has left only cello music on the music stand, which looks ridiculously complicated.

He picks up the guitar and plays.

OCTOBER 10. FRIDAY.

Lyla Marks's House; 7:02 a.m.

The newspaper is open to the Arts page, and Lyla's face is smiling in the featured photo.

> Young cellist Lyla Marks is among the four talented string players chosen for solo concerts in the Kennedy Center's Young Strings program.

"Good morning, Star!" Her dad brings two glasses of orange juice to the table.

Lyla's stomach sinks.

Her dad looks at the newspaper over her shoulder.

"I'm so glad we did that photo shoot. Didn't it turn out great?"

Lyla nods. She manages to smile and eat her breakfast, listening to her father go on and on about what this will mean, how he'll call Coles and let them know, how they'll be certain to want to schedule an audition.

Later, when she gets into Annie's car, Mrs. Win smiles nervously and congratulates her, and Annie doesn't say a word. As soon as they arrive at school and get out of the car, Annie erupts.

"Why didn't you tell me you made it? You must have been perfect. Were you perfect?"

Lyla doesn't answer.

Annie pushes through the school doors. "I was better than the idiot who went before me."

"Violins had more competition."

"Shut up."

"It's true, Annie."

"I know what's going to happen."

"What do you mean?"

"I'm not going to make it into Coles and you are."

"Stop it."

"I hate you. Stop making every audition."

"Please stop saying that, Annie."

Annie storms ahead.

Kenneth Chan yells to Lyla, "Hey, I saw your picture in the paper!"

Lyla wishes she could go home.

All morning, Annie avoids her. Finally, the lunch break arrives, and by the time Lyla gets to the practice room, she is almost shaking. She closes the door and sits with her face in her hands.

After a few minutes, she pulls out a piece of paper and a pen and begins to write.

Dear Mr. Odd,
   I lied. You blew me away when you asked me if playing the cello makes me happy. Nobody has ever asked me that, and it seems profound, and I didn't answer you honestly because the truth is I'm not happy.
   When I was playing the solo during the school assembly, I <u>was</u> a machine. I played all the right notes, and all day people kept saying how great it was. But something was wrong, and I didn't even let myself admit it. Then I got your note. Thrumming. That's interesting. I don't think I'm thrumming a lot right now. I want a break from the cello, but I feel guilty about that.
   —Ms. Even

She doesn't know if writing makes her feel better or worse. She sets the paper and pen down and plays through the scales on the guitar until the end of the period. Then she rushes out and slips the note into Tripp's locker before she loses her nerve.

Dear Ms. Even,

I'm in English right now. I stopped at my locker after lunch and found your note. I'm going to put this in your locker after class. I thought you might want to get a reply before having to wait until Monday rolls around.

Yesterday, I was at the store—ever go to Broody's Rug + Carpet? Well, it's our store. I had to go there after school yesterday, and there was this mom and this kindergarten kid looking at rugs for the kid's room. And the kid picked out this pomegranate-colored rug with all these colorful swooshes and he called it the "blasty rug," and the mom kept pulling him over to this plain brown rug and saying, "This will match your bedspread, Henry." My mom kept saying how nice brown is because it doesn't show dirt. And Henry kept going back to the "blasty" rug and tracing the swooshes with his finger, making different sounds for each one, like that's what the rug sounded like to him. And then Henry's mom bought the brown rug behind his back and then she said, "Come on, Henry honey. You're going to love this."

I know it's going to sound morbid, but I had this negative fantasy that Henry died and the mom was eaten alive by guilt because she didn't buy him the blasty rug, and then I felt guilty about fantasizing that a kid dies. I know. There's something wrong with me. But there's something wrong with moms who think they know what is right for their kids. Maybe the blasty rug was the perfect rug for him, a magic carpet. Maybe he would sit on it whenever he was feeling sad and it would make him feel better. Why do moms smile and lie and say they know what's good for you?

Tell your parents you want to take a break from the cello. Tell them you want to play guitar. No guilt allowed.

—Mr. Odd

P.S. By the way, scales are good, but maybe you need to pick up the guitar and let yourself experiment. Start with one note and let your fingers find a *place to go; and if you like the tune, repeat it until it wants to go somewhere new, then follow it, even if it peregrinates. This message has been brought to you by The National Peregrination Society.*

ROCKLAND HALLWAY; 3:16 P.M.

Lyla is reading Tripp's letter at her locker when Annie shows up. Reluctantly, she slips the note into her backpack and shifts the backpack to her other shoulder.

"I have decided to forget about the Kennedy Center thing," Annie says. "I think we need to focus on the talent show. I just heard that Brittany and three other girls are calling themselves the Canticle Quartet and they signed up for the five thirty audition slot."

Lyla tries to focus on what Annie is saying, but she wants to be alone with the letter, to read it again without interruption.

"Did you hear me?" Annie says. "I'm talking about the auditions for the talent show. We have the three twenty slot, which I think is bad. By the time the auditions are over, Jacoby will have forgotten how good we are. Let's go see if we can change ours."

"Stop obsessing. Just leave it the way it is."

Annie frowns. "I'm not obsessing. I'm strategizing.

Okay. Let's go to my house and practice first and then we have to make banana bread for the bake sale. Text your dad right now. My mom is on her way."

"Stop telling me what I have to do!" Lyla snaps.

Annie makes a face. "What is wrong with you?"

"Nothing."

"You're so lying."

"I'm . . . I'm just not feeling good today."

Annie's eyes flash. "It's the article, isn't it?"

"What are you talking about?"

"That newspaper article. Now that you're famous, you don't want to do a duet for the talent show, do you?"

"No! That's not it. I'm not feeling good," Lyla says. "I have to go to the bathroom. Just go with your mom. I'll call you later."

"You can't be sick," Annie calls after her. "I'm trying to get past the Kennedy Center thing, Lyla. The least you can do is help me out here. You're coming over tonight."

Lyla bites the inside of her cheek to keep from screaming. "I'll call you later," she says without looking. She walks into a girls' restroom and reads Tripp's letter three times in a row.

ROCKLAND HALLWAY; 3:19 P.M.

Tripp is walking down the hallway, looking for a glimpse of Lyla even though, if he saw her, he wouldn't

85

know what to say. He can't wait until Monday when he can play in the little room again and find, hopefully, another note.

His phone buzzes. A text message from an unfamiliar number.

This is Benjamin Fick. I am your peer tutor. We'll meet Mondays and Wednesdays at 11:30. Resource Rm. See you Mon.

Tripp stares at the screen of his cell phone. The Termite did it. She signed him up and gave his cell phone number. He wishes there was a phone number he could call: IS YOUR MOTHER A TERMITE? CALL 1-800-555-5555 AND WE'LL GET HER OUT OF YOUR LIFE!

Lyla's Room; 5:00 p.m.

Lyla crawls into bed the minute she is home. She tells her dad she's sick and she texts Annie with the news that she can't come over.

"Head or stomach?" her dad says, touching her forehead.

"Head. Ache, but no fever."

"Well, hopefully, by tomorrow morning you'll be right as rain so you don't miss your Metz Youth Orchestra rehearsal." He pats her leg. "I'll bring you up a strawberry smoothie. Does that sound good?"

She nods, and he leaves.

Her cell phone buzzes. A text from Annie.

Annie/Get well fast. Tomorrow let's practice after MYO rehearsal. You can't say no.

Lyla/Sure. See you tomorrow.

Lyla turns off her phone. Tomorrow morning, she will wake up and go to MYO and then practice for the talent show with Annie. Already, she is dreading it.

OCTOBER 13. MONDAY.

ROCKLAND HALLWAY; 11:21 A.M.

After the bell rings, dismissing Tripp from Spanish, his cell phone buzzes.

> **Mom/**don't forget tutor session in resource room.
> **Tripp/**you're not supposed to text during school.
> **Mom/**I know your schedule. It's lunch. go to tutor.
> **Tripp/**fine. I'm turning off phone.

Tripp puts his phone in his pocket and reluctantly heads toward the resource room. His feet are heavy. The guitar, waiting for him in the little room, acts like an invisible magnet. He can't fight it. He pulls out his cell phone and sends a message to Benjamin Fick:

Tripp/severe abdominal cramping. going to health room. sorry.

In a perfect world, he would not lie. He would not need to.

He hurries to the music room. As soon as he closes the door to the little room, he feels better. It's like every other part of his life is a bad dream and this is the only part that's real.

The last flurry of notes between Lyla and him was in their lockers, so that means a letter in the guitar case is unlikely, but he opens the guitar case and there it is: another note. He sits on the floor to read it.

Dear Mr. Odd,
Surprise and Happy Monday. I have orchestra first period, so I slipped in here to put this note inside the guitar case.
I love what you wrote about that boy and the blasty rug. I wish his mom had let him get it.
I hope you don't mind this, but I'm going to tell you anyway. I've always wondered about you. I mean, you were basically this nice normal smart kid. You were in my math class in sixth grade, remember? Anyway, you and that one kid were always doing stuff together and then he

moved away. Right after that, you didn't show up, and everybody heard about your dad. When you came back, I wanted to say something like sorry because I kept thinking about how hard it would be to lose a dad and a best friend kind of at the same time. But we didn't know each other and you can't just go up to someone and say sorry. And I didn't know if it would make you feel better or worse. But I just wanted to say it anyway. That's all.

—Ms. Even

P.S. Thanks for the advice to experiment. I will try it out tomorrow when it's my turn in the little room.

P.P.S. I have never eaten a pomegranate. Have you?

The note feels alive in his hands, like a bird with a beating heart. He reads it again, hardly daring to breathe, lingering on the words *sorry* and *dad*. He didn't even know that he needed to hear these words, but somehow Lyla Marks knew.

He pulls out the guitar. Tomorrow, Lyla will be right here with this guitar in her hands, and instead of practicing scales, she will just play, and maybe that will make her happy. The idea of this makes a song leap out of him: an odd melody bouncing out. He repeats the parts he likes and experiments with the parts that don't work. He plays it over and over, shaping it each time. The "Mr. Odd" song.

Deep into it, there's a thump on the wall and Annie Win yells: "Too loud!"

He laughs and keeps playing. After a while, the bell rings, announcing the end of lunch. Reluctantly, Tripp stops. He wants to leave a note, but he doesn't have any paper and he doesn't want to write anything on the note she left for him.

He takes a pen out of his back pocket. On the curve of the guitar, the part that she will see when she is holding it, he tries writing, but the ink smears off. Using his pen like an engraving tool, he scratches two words into the lacquer: *Just play*.

On the way out, his phone buzzes.

Fick/Hi! Sorry about the abdominal trouble. See you Wed.

Oh joy.

OCTOBER 14. TUESDAY.

Practice Room B; 11:26 a.m.

No note tucked between the strings when Lyla opens the guitar case. But when she sets it on her lap, she sees the message scratched into the side—*Just play*—and it lights her up.

She takes a deep breath. She lets her fingers wander around randomly plucking out different combinations of notes until, by accident, she finds something she likes. She repeats it. She plays with it until she has a phrase, the beginning of a melody, and then another phrase and another. She closes her eyes and tries to let the music come through her, when the door opens.

Annie walks in, her violin case in hand, and stares. "What are you doing?"

Lyla's heart pounds. "It's an even day. Why are you here?"

"I'm sneaking in so we can practice our duet."

"That's against the rules."

"Jacoby won't know. He took the beginning orchestra on that field trip. What are you doing?"

Lyla looks down at the guitar in her hands and tries to shrug it off. "It was here and so I just picked it up." She puts it back in the case. "I don't think being here is a good idea, Annie. Remember last year when those two girls broke the rule?"

"They were smoking! We'd just be playing music."

"Rules are rules. Really. I think you should go." Lyla lowers her voice. "Patricia Kent will tell on us. Seriously. And aren't you doing that lunchtime tutoring thing?"

"Just once a week." Annie frowns. "Come on, we need to practice. You didn't want to sleep over on Friday. You were crabby on Saturday. You never want to practice."

"I was sick! We have three whole weeks 'til the talent show audition, Annie."

"You sound like you're doing me this huge favor by letting me play with you."

"That is not fair. That's not what I sound like. Two people are not allowed in practice rooms. I don't like breaking rules. That's all."

"Fine, I'm leaving." Annie storms out, slamming the door.

Heart pounding, Lyla sits. Why does every interaction with Annie leave her feeling guilty? Is it wrong for her to want some time to herself?

She checks outside to make sure Annie is gone, then she gets the guitar out again. It takes a while for the room to feel like hers again, but slowly she begins to calm down and feel the connection to the music. Once she finds it, she doesn't want any intrusions. She hears a melody, and a line of lyrics pops into her head. *"All I want is a little room to play . . ."* she sings. Not bad. She keeps at it until the period ends, too quickly. As she puts away the guitar and walks down the hall, her song keeps playing inside her head. *Now I've got myself a little room to play. . . .*

Annie appears around a corner, and Lyla runs over and hugs her. "Don't be grumpy, Annie!"

Annie pulls away and keeps walking.

"Come on, Annie, we've got the talent show duet down—"

"I don't think you get it, Lyla." Annie stops, her eyes hot and teary. "It's easy for you to say, oh, we don't need to practice. You made the Kennedy Center audition. I didn't." She walks on.

"I'm sorry, Annie. On Friday, I'll come over and we will practice our duet and we will NAIL it." She grabs Annie's arm and smiles. "What do you want to wear for the audition?"

Annie smiles reluctantly. "Something new."

"We can go shopping together," Lyla says.

"Okay. But not today. We have Sweet Tooth and then we need to study for the physics unit quiz."

Lyla twirls. "The answer to every question is Force equals Mass times Acceleration. I love science."

"I can't believe you like Mr. Sanders. He has hairy arms."

Lyla laughs.

Annie's eyes widen. "Lyla, he's looking at you," she whispers.

Lyla looks around.

"Don't look," Annie whispers. "Tripp Broody."

Lyla catches a glimpse of Tripp before Annie turns her away. She wants to tell him that she wrote a song, that she *played*. "He's not looking at me, Annie. He's walking down the hall."

"He saw you twirl. What class did you say you have with him?"

Lyla tries to make her voice sound casual. "I don't have a class with him."

"Yesterday, he was playing way too loud."

Lyla laughs.

Annie pushes her. "Why didn't you say hi just now? Has he left you any more notes?"

"Leave me alone, Annie."

"I'm glad you didn't. He's too weird. I saw his name on the schedule for peer tutoring. Benjamin Fick is tutoring him. I think he might be brain damaged."

"Annie!"

"*Pardon moi* for telling the truth." She waves and disappears into the stairwell to go to her next class.

He is not brain damaged, Lyla wants to say. He is . . . just a bit odd. In a really interesting way.

OCTOBER 15. WEDNESDAY.

PRACTICE ROOM B; 11:37 A.M.

Tripp is in the practice room, convinced that the peer-tutor police will burst onto the scene at any moment with Benjamin Fick and seize him. But how could he possibly concentrate on Newton's laws or graphing coordinates or calculating the standard deviation from the norm with the little room waiting for him?

When he opens the guitar case, he is disappointed to find no note tucked between the strings. But Ms. Even has left a piece of paper under the guitar: notes for a song.

Little Room Song

Chorus!

Now I've got myself

A little room to play

~~I will play all day~~

All my worries will fade away

As soon as I start to play

Start on DB
Go to EC
Then move up 2 frets

~~Get ready, it's time for a test~~

Fill in the blank, it's time for a test

As soon as I'm done, it's on to the next

Tests - multiple choice
          true or false
          pressure!

Pressures
time
schedule
always being
perfect

True or false, choose the one that's best

(Start singing on B)

Inspired, he writes her a message.

Dear Ms. Even,
   I hope you don't mind that I read the notebook page you left underneath the guitar. It looks like you're brainstorming a song? I want to hear it. I noticed that you tried writing out the notes you're playing. Guitar players either write chords or what's called tablature. You might find it easier to make chord diagrams. Here's an example.

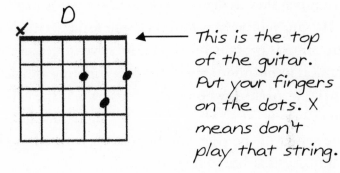

This is the top of the guitar. Put your fingers on the dots. X means don't play that string.

   As for pomegranates, I think the only part you eat is the seeds, and I don't think I've ever eaten an actual seed, but I don't know for sure. Yesterday after school, I did some research on pomegranates when I should have been *working on my history report. The pomegranate is called la granada in Spanish. In French, it's called la grenade, which makes me think of hand grenades, and pomegranates do sort of look like hand grenades. They are full of nutrients and antioxidants which are good for us, whatever those are. So maybe they are like healthy grenades. If I were a doctor, I would lob them at sick people.*

    —Mr. Odd

Tripp picks up the guitar. Something good is happening. He can feel it in the guitar. He can feel it in the little room. Strands of thought twine themselves together into a decision in his mind. He'll stop peregrinating and actually write words for a whole song of his own. If she can do it, he can do it. The "Mr. Odd" song. He writes the title in the center of the page and brainstorms everything he can think of that has to do with it.

Then he plays the melody that has been bouncing around in his brain lately and under his breath. He pulls out the parts from his brainstorm that he likes and he experiments.

i can hear
ODD THINGS fear
here
clear
superhuman cilia mirror
cilia
iris
eyes/ears
oddness
oddity

i'm odd   not logical
abnormal   illogical
unnormal

look at
ME

MR. ODD

remediation

norm
form
warm

standard deviation
away from the norm

form
shape
w/0

always
deviating
away from
the norm

free radical
my problems can't
be reduced to
X, Y, or Z

no rational solutions for my x,y,z

a graph without coordinates!

logic can't fix what's
wrong with me

1,3,5,7,9
IT'S AN ODD DAY
I'M IN AN ODD WAY

He sings:

> *I'm a graph without coordinates,*
> *A shape without form,*
> *Always deviating away from the norm.*
> *Logic can't fix what's wrong with me.*
> *I'm odd. I'm odd. I'm odd.*
> *Indeed.*

He laughs. It's a start.

PRACTICE ROOM HALLWAY; 11:56 A.M.

Lyla tiptoes past Practice Room A and listens. Annie's violin is loud and clear. Lyla shifts over to Practice Room B and listens. Tripp is singing! She grins and leans in, her ear close to the door.

Just after Lyla notices that Annie's violin has stopped, the sound of Annie's shriek comes. The door to Room A opens and Annie flies out.

"Lyla! I was coming to get you. My mom just texted about Coles. You heard, didn't you?"

In a flash, Lyla knows what must have happened. It's all over Annie's face. Her mom must have texted her with the news that Coles has accepted her application and wants to schedule an audition. Annie must think that Lyla received the same great news and was coming to find her.

Annie grabs her in a hug.

The guitar playing in Practice Room B has stopped.

"I knew we'd make it, Lyla!" She grabs Lyla again and spins around, laughing.

Lyla tries to steady herself, noticing the door to Practice Room B is open a crack.

"Isn't it great?" Annie says. "How come you're not smiling?"

"I'm in shock," Lyla says. "Yeah, it's great." She forces out a smile.

THE METRO; 4:43 P.M.

"I waited for you." Benjamin Fick's voice sounds like he swallowed sandpaper.

"My bad," Tripp says into the phone. "No offense, but I will die if I get tutored." There's silence on the other end, so Tripp adds, "Best of luck helping other math-challenged people. Really."

"Ms. Kettering knows you didn't show," Benjamin says. "She said that if you don't show again, she'll call you and your mom in for a conference."

Tripp is in too good of a mood to let even this bring him down. He smiles. "Tell Kettering that we're meeting in the cafeteria because I like the smell of rancid meat. I'll study on my own and boost my grades to make you look good. It's a win-win."

There is a moment of silence while Benjamin considers becoming an accessory to this crime. "Fine," Benjamin says, and hangs up.

Fine is fine is fine, indeed.

OCTOBER 16. THURSDAY.

Practice Room B; 11:24 a.m.

Annie has been talking nonstop about Coles ever since yesterday. Finally, Lyla's time in the practice room arrives. When she closes the door, the silence is so peaceful, it makes her want to cry. She opens the guitar case and smiles to see another letter. Tripp wants to hear her song.

She calls up the recording program on the computer and plugs in the microphone. Last year, Ms. Peabody taught her how to make a recording so that she could analyze her progress on solos; she never thought she'd be using it to record herself singing and playing the guitar. She picks up the guitar and hits the record button and then stares at the screen, not sure if she can really do it.

Tripp might not like the song or the sound of her voice. She takes a breath and tells herself that she is just going to record it for herself, to hear what it sounds like. She starts again. Halfway through, she makes her first mistake and stops. It takes three tries, but she finally gets through it without making a noticeable mistake. Before she has a chance to regret it, she searches the web for Tripp Broody, finds his efriends page, and sends him a message.

<To: Tripp Broody> October 16
[Attach: LittleRoomSong.MP3]

Hey Tripp, you wanted to hear my song, so I recorded it and attached it.

She decides to add something else to the message, so that it's not just the song. That way, if he doesn't like the song, he'll have something else to comment about.

BTW, did you hear Annie screaming yesterday? We have been invited to audition for this school in Boston called Coles Conservatory of Music. Great music school. Grades 10–12. You live in dorms and they have teachers for all the regular classes, like math and science, but half the day is devoted to music. If you go there, you basically know you're going to make it as a pro. Annie and I made this pact to apply, but now every time I think about it, I get panicky. I don't think I want to audition for it anymore, but there's no way I can get out of it.

—Ms. Even

Done.

She takes another breath and hits SEND.

ROCKLAND HALLWAY, 3:11 P.M.

Tripp's afternoon classes crawl by. The thought of doing homework and spending the evening listening to the Termite drone makes him want to lie down in the middle of the hallway and be trampled by the herds. Why can't the Winds of Fate blow something interesting in his direction, he wonders, to prevent him from succumbing to the slow death of boredom?

As soon as he is dismissed from his last class, he pulls out his cell phone. He can't quite believe what he's seeing. There is a message in his efriends in-box: Lyla Marks has sent him a song.

He's desperate to hear it, but he doesn't want the noises of the hallway to compete. Quickly, he grabs his books out of his locker and leaves.

He runs to the Metro, catches the subway headed uptown, and settles in a seat. He adjusts his earbuds and opens the MP3 file.

This pure sound streams into his ears: the guitar first, then Lyla's voice dancing out neatly, line after line.

> *Fill in the blank, it's time for a test.*
> *Soon as I'm done, it's on to the next.*
> *True or false, just choose the one that's best,*
> *Through the halls, I'm running out of breath.*

> *But now I've got myself a little room to play,*
> *Now I've got myself a little room to play,*
> *All my worries fade away*
> *As soon as I start to play.*

> *Someone measures every step of mine,*
> *A to B straight down the line.*
> *Everybody's waiting all the while.*
> *I'm supposed to show up and smile.*

> *But now I've got myself a little room to play,*
> *Now I've got myself a little room to play,*
> *All my worries fade away*
> *As soon as I start to play.*

> *Now no one's watching me,*
> *No one hears.*
> *I walk into the room*
> *and I disappear.*

Why do I choose this way to follow?
All the answers are due tomorrow.
Everybody's waiting all the while.
Maybe I won't show up and smile.

'Cause I've got myself a little room to play,
Now I've got myself a little room to play,
All my worries fade away . . . they fade away
As soon as I start to play.

As soon as Tripp gets home, he downloads Lyla's MP3 to his laptop, puts on his headphones, and listens to it again.

<To: Lyla Marks> October 16

Ms. Even: How do I describe your song? When I was about eight, we were driving to this property we have in the woods, and we were passing through a small town, and this squirrel caught my eye. We were at a stop sign and the squirrel was on a telephone pole next to our car. As we started going, it started running next to us . . . just this effortless, beautiful squirrel gallop along a tightrope of telephone wire. When it reached the next pole, and the next, it kept going, like it was keeping me company. I wanted to tell my dad to look, but I thought that might break the spell and the squirrel might stop. That's how I felt when I listened to your song. I loved it.—Mr. Odd

<To: Tripp Broody> October 16

That means a lot. Thanks. I want to hear one of your songs.

Tripp looks at himself in the mirror. She wants to hear one of his songs. What has he gotten himself into? He can't do this. He makes a face. Then he grabs a pencil and holds it like a microphone. "*I'm going to sing a song for you*," he sings. Then he stops. "No, I'm not," he says, and chucks the pencil across the room. It bounces off the wall and lands on his pillow. He sounds ridiculous. He cannot do this. He goes back to his computer. Another message pops up.

<To: Tripp Broody> October 16

Hey, what's your cell number in case I need to call. . . .

She wants his cell number? Is she going to actually call him sometime and expect him to be able to talk? He runs his fingers through his hair. Then he sits down. *No problem*, he says to himself, *just type in your number and hit* SEND. He takes a deep breath in, does it, and lets the breath out. Why was that so scary?

110

OCTOBER 17. FRIDAY.

PRACTICE ROOM B; 11:27 A.M.

Odd day. Tripp's got the little room. From his pocket, he pulls a list that he made and sets it on the music stand, just in case.

> *Things to say if Ms. E actually calls*
> *The blasty rug you ordered is in.*
> *Have you ever had your appendix removed?*
> *How do you think Western Civilization will end?*

He gets out his guitar and tries to concentrate. He

wants to finish his song. He wants to have the guts to record it for Lyla.

ROCKLAND HALLWAY; 3:14 P.M.

Lyla leans against her locker and looks at Tripp's name in her contact list. All she has to do is press CALL.

Funny. She can play all the right notes on the cello in front of six Kennedy Center judges and she can't get her finger to press CALL. Send a text—that'll be easier.

> Hey, Mr. Odd. What're you doing?

She puts Tripp's name in the "to" box and hits SEND just as Annie screeches behind her.

"Did I just see Tripp Broody's name?" Annie tries to grab her phone.

"Don't be so grabby."

"You were sending him a text!"

"Is that illegal?" Lyla quickly pockets her phone.

"What's going on with you and Tripp Broody?"

"Nothing." She turns and busies herself putting folders she doesn't need into her backpack. "He asked about a math assignment."

"Why?

Lyla stands up and closes her locker. "We ran into each other in the hall and—I don't know—he asked me about math and I said I'll text you."

"So you're best friends with Tripp Broody?"

"I've had a total of one conversation. Stop making such a big deal about it."

"No."

"Yes."

"No."

"Yes."

"Promise you're not going to hang out with him."

"Okay. Okay."

"Good. Okay. What are you doing tonight? Hot date with Tripp? Just kidding. My mom said since we have to be back at school at seven, you can just stay for dinner."

"What?"

"We'll practice all our music and then we can make the poster and eat dinner. Then my mom can take us back for the bake sale."

"I forgot about that."

"What do you mean you forgot?"

"I mean I forgot."

"We get beaucoup community service points for this. What's wrong with you, Lyla? Our poster has to be better than Marisse's. We're voting for president next week." Annie's phone buzzes. "My mom is in the parking lot. Come on."

"I'll meet you down there. I left my science notebook in Sanders's room. I have to run and get it."

Annie shakes her head. "You're officially losing your mind. Hurry up."

Lyla heads toward the science hallway, turning to watch Annie run in the opposite direction. When Annie is out of sight, she opens her phone. He has texted back.

Tripp/hi even. i'm texting you.
Lyla/no way.
Tripp/ok. I'm not.

Lyla presses CALL. He doesn't answer.

She ends the call.

Three seconds later her phone rings.

"Hi," she says, and winces. Kind of a lame way to start.

"This is Broody's Rug and Carpet. That blasty rug you ordered is ready for pickup."

She laughs.

"That's my opening line," he says. "I worked on that all night."

"I like it. Hey, did you really like my song?" She winces again. Why did she ask that? It sounds like she's trying to get a compliment.

"Indeed," he says.

She smiles, her mouth making a little sound, and she wonders if he heard it. "Now it's your turn to do a song," she says quickly.

"I'm a formless meanderer."

"Lame excuse."

"I don't sing."

"Liar. I heard you."

"When?"

"Wednesday. Practice room."

"What! Were you spying? I was NOT singing."

"You were humming along. Jacoby does that when he's into it."

"Are you stalking me?"

"You have a good voice. You sound like hot chocolate."

"Your ear cilia aren't working."

"Ha."

"I sound like a wounded aardvark."

"I had an aardvark when I was young!"

"You have got to be kidding."

"Not a real one. A small fuzzy one. It had big ears. My mom brought it back for me from some trip she took."

"Most kids have teddy bears. Having an aardvark is so odd . . . it's actually . . . *un*even."

She laughs. "I don't know what ever happened to it. I loved that aardvark. What does an aardvark sound like anyway?"

"Like me trying to sing."

"You're not an aardvark; you're a chicken."

"You are insulting my aardvarkian ancestors."

She laughs again. "Where are you?"

"Outside on the wall by the maple tree. Where are you?"

"Science hallway."

"Are you coming out?" He sounds nervous.

"I have to meet Annie."

"Okay. Talk to you later—"

"Wait. When can I pick up my blasty rug?"

He laughs.

"I want to hear your song soon," she adds.

"Okay."

TRIPP'S HOUSE; 6:33 P.M.

Tripp is standing at the kitchen sink, eating leftover Chinese food out of the carton. Soy sauce spills onto the counter, and his mom wipes it up.

She tosses the sponge in the sink and carries a basket filled with small bottles of sparkling water to the dining room and sets it next to a plate of brownies.

"What are you going to do tonight?" She comes back into the kitchen and pulls the coffeepot out of the coffeemaker.

"Well, if I had my guitar . . ." He looks out the window. The sun is setting. The sky is drained of color, with only a hint of orange at the horizon. He wants to finish his song and practice it a thousand times until it's good enough to record.

She rolls her eyes. "Please don't start this now, Tripp."

He puts down his fork. "I have gone forty-six days

116

without it. I am forty-six times closer to insanity."

She fills up the pot and pours it into the coffeemaker. "You can't see it, but that guitar has been nothing but trouble."

"What?"

"It was okay at first, but then you started isolating yourself. Every day after school. All day Saturday and Sunday—"

"I had nothing else to do. Josh moved away."

"Exactly. You should have been out making new friends. And then your grades started sliding and they've been downhill ever since. You have been using it to waste your time when—"

"Just because you don't value music doesn't mean I shouldn't be able to play. I don't tell you that I think you're wasting your time on whatever it is you're doing tonight."

She groans. "This is called duty." She flips on the coffeemaker and grabs a stack of small white napkins. "Susan signed me up to be chairperson for the Slater Creek Parkway Cleanup Committee, and I'm too nice to back out, so I'm hosting the meeting." She walks the napkins into the dining room and calls back. "And I do value music."

He feels a pang of guilt about the cleanup committee, but it is quickly replaced by anger. "You do not."

She storms back into the kitchen, hand on her hip. "You think I'm a monster."

He grabs his coat and walks past her to the front door.

"What are you doing?" she asks.

"Bike ride," he says.

"No way."

"I finished my homework."

"It's dark—"

"I have a light." He opens the front door just as a woman is about to knock.

"Cindy!" his mom chirps. "Welcome, welcome!"

"Hi, Terry!" the woman chirps back. "Oh my Lord, is this Tripp? You've grown!"

"Indeed," Tripp says. "Miraculously, the local termites have not stunted my growth."

The woman's laugh has a hollow ring.

"I'm going for a ride on Slater Creek Parkway," he adds. "As a user of the bike path, I thank you in advance for your committee's cleanup efforts."

The woman thinks this is hilarious.

His mom fakes a smile and calls out: "Be careful and wear your helmet, Tripp."

In the cool air, Tripp rides to the parkway, a road that follows a narrow creek with a thin strip of woods on either side. He breathes in the muddy smell of the creek and the woods, a rich smell that reminds him of his dad, and his throat closes. A thought emerges: *I wish it had been Mom instead of Dad.* As soon as he thinks it, he fears lightning will strike. It's horrible, but true.

As he coasts down a hill, he sees a young deer in the

grassy area between the picnic tables and small parking lot, her head bent, nibbling the grass.

Tripp holds his breath and starts to brake. Farther beyond the deer, he sees an approaching car on the road. The deer raises her head, the patch of fur at her neck so white, and she looks right at Tripp. Her ears twitch. "Please don't be spooked," Tripp whispers.

The deer bolts away from Tripp and leaps onto the road. The car screeches and swerves. Tripp sees the flash of the deer's tail as she makes it to the other side and disappears into the shadows of someone's backyard. The car passes by, and the road is quiet again.

Tripp's heart is pounding. He stands for a long minute, straddling his bike, feeling like he is the one who just escaped being hit. He wants to call Lyla and tell her what just happened, talk to her about how sad it is when you see a deer in such a crowded area because they have no place to go. He has this feeling that she would understand, but what if she thought it was strange that he called out of the blue? He rides on and, when he gets to the stoplight, turns onto the busy street. The pawnshop is just five blocks up; the guitar he noticed the last time he passed is still in the window, propped against an ugly green chair. After he locks up his bike, he walks in and asks the big bald guy behind the counter if he can see the guitar.

"You just want to play it or are you actually interested in buying?" the guy asks, without moving.

"I'm interested in buying," Tripp says.

The guy gets it for him, and Tripp plays until the guy says it's closing time already and he gets kicked out.

OCTOBER 18. SATURDAY.

Bank of America; 10:01 a.m.

Tripp walks into the Bank of America and looks around. He has been to the bank only two or three times his entire life, and he's not entirely sure how it works. Four people are waiting in line to see one of the three women who are sitting behind windows. Tripp joins the line, pulling out the black book that has his account number and deposit and withdrawal forms. While he waits for his turn, his phone buzzes and he grins.

Lyla/Hey what's up?

Lyla texting out of the blue. Nice surprise indeed.

Tripp/I'm at the bank.

Lyla/Robbing it?

Tripp/taking out money I saved. gonna buy a guitar.

Lyla/Cool! Hey how did you learn to play if you don't have one?

Tripp/I have one but my mom confiscated it.

Lyla/harsh

Tripp/she locked it in a closet at her store.

Lyla/steal it back

Tripp/honking lock on it.

Lyla/wait. won't your mom be mad if you buy one?

Tripp/beds are meant to hide things under

Lyla/Good luck with that. I gotta go. I'm on a break at MYO rehearsal.

Tripp/What's MYO? The Merry Yogurt Organization?

Lyla/Metz Youth Orchestra. Bye.

"Next," the woman on the end says.

He steps up, slips the form under the glass partition, and smiles.

"Photo ID," the teller says.

Tripp wasn't expecting that. He pulls his school ID out of his pocket while she looks at the form and taps something into the computer. After a moment, she slips the form back to him. "Sorry, I can't process this. It's a minor account and the custodian"—she checks the screen—"Terry Broody, has essentially placed a freeze on it."

"A freeze?"

"You can't withdraw funds without her signature."

"She can't do that. It's my money."

"The way the account is set up, she can. Sorry." She gives him a fake smile. She isn't sorry at all.

He leaves and rides back home.

Depressed, he opens up the desk drawer in the kitchen and slips his black book back in. Her checkbook catches his eye. He takes it and hides it in the back of the freezer, underneath a bag of frozen lima beans. If she can freeze his account, he can freeze hers.

Tripp's Room; 12:47 P.M.

<To: Lyla Marks> October 18

I couldn't get a guitar. My mom froze my bank account. I'm beyond mad.—Mr. Odd

<To: Tripp Broody> October 18

I'm so sorry! Maybe you should write a song about it.

<To: Lyla Marks> October 18

Ode to Rage. IF I HAD MY GUITAR I'D BE FINE.

<To: Tripp Broody> October 18

You know how in that note you said, tell your parents you want to take a break from the cello? Well, there's only my dad. My mom died when I was six. She was a cellist and she performed all over the world and she was on a flight going from one country to another and something went wrong and the airplane went down in the ocean. It was weird—there wasn't room on that flight for her cello because of some mix-up and she had agreed to have it sent on the next flight. I remember my dad crying when the cello was delivered.

When I got older I thought the fact that the cello survived was like a sign that I was supposed to play it. When you and I first started exchanging notes, I thought we had nothing in common, but we are sort of living parallel lives. We both have one parent, and we both don't have any brothers or sisters, and we both feel pressured even though it's in different ways.

I think your mom is insane to take away the one thing that makes you feel sane. Why don't they get it? It's like the blasty rug. Okay. This is ridiculously long.—Ms. Even

<To: Lyla Marks> October 18

It is weird how we have so much in common. One

day you had a mom and the next day you didn't. Same with me. One day he was my normal dad and then a blood vessel inside his brain exploded and he was dead. Sometimes I look at myself in the mirror and imagine my brain exploding. Do you ever have morbid thoughts?

<To: Tripp Broody> October 18

Sometimes I imagine my cello exploding. And sometimes I look at myself in the mirror, and my own face looks like a mask to me.

<To: Lyla Marks> October 18

When I ride the Metro, and it goes under, I stare at my reflection in the window and it's like a dark ghost version of me is whooshing along at the exact same speed outside the train. And it's like, "Who are you?"

Okay, here's something else weird about me. You know how I said that the kid (Henry) had a connection with the blasty rug, like he was hearing the rug's vibe and humming along with it? Well, I have a Vibe Theory. Ever since I can remember, I've felt like everything has a vibe, which I could sense. Inanimate things, like socks and pencils and stuff. Hard to explain, but I would look at a bunch of pencils and one would call out to me, "Pick me! I'm the happy pencil!"

<To: Tripp Broody> October 18

That's funny. I've always tried to hear things that I shouldn't be able to hear. You know how dogs can hear a high-pitched whistle and we can't? Annie just reminded me how I thought I could hear my bones grow in the fifth grade. Speaking of hearing things . . . Did you write a song? If so, I could come to the practice room at lunch tomorrow and you could play it for me. Okie-dokie?

<To: Lyla Marks> October 18

I did write a song, but no okie-dokie on coming to the practice room. I'm not good at in-person stuff.

<To: Tripp Broody> October 18

Bawk bawk.

<To: Lyla Marks> October 18

I'm not a chicken. I'm an aardvark. Remember? I'm just finishing the lyrics. I haven't even had a chance to play it with guitar.

<To: Tripp Broody> October 18

Okay. Monday is an even day. You can have the

practice room at lunch, but you have to record your
song and send me the MP3.

<To: Lyla Marks> October 18

   Deal.

He can't believe he has just agreed to record and send
his song. Tripp steps away from the computer and looks
at himself in the mirror to confirm the truth: Yes, he
looks absolutely insane.

OCTOBER 19. SUNDAY.

TRIPP'S ROOM; 7:13 P.M.

Tripp is singing when his mom walks in with a plate of warm brownies.

"Were you singing?" she asks.

"Are those brownies?" A deft subject change.

"Superchunk chocolate." She smiles, obviously unaware of the fact that her checkbook is currently on ice. "I thought you might need something to keep you going," she says. "Your Intro to Tech teacher finally put up the review sheet on Edline. And there's a new physics worksheet posted. How's that unit going?"

Fie, villain! I see right through your wily ways, he thinks. *Mere melted chocolate will not warm my heart toward the*

tedious task ahead. Nor will it warm my heart toward you,
O Termite in Residence.

She hands him the plate. He is craving a scoop of vanilla ice cream for the warm brownies, but he doesn't dare bring attention to the freezer, where the checkbook is hidden. He breaks a brownie in half and stuffs it into his mouth.

"How are your tutor sessions going?"

Pang of guilt. He chews and swallows. "Well, Benjamin Fick is certainly a nice young man," he says.

"That tone." She shakes her head. "There is no need for sarcasm. He's probably nice."

"Indeed. Sarcasm is the enemy of the people."

His mom sighs and starts to leave. "By the way, have you seen my checkbook?"

Superchunk pang of guilt. "I am not allowed to bank. I believe that includes writing checks."

Her glance is full of suspicion. "It was right where I always keep it."

Tripp shrugs, mouth full.

You scream. I scream. We all scream for frozen things.

OCTOBER 20. MONDAY.

PRACTICE ROOM B; 11:23 A.M.

How odd it feels to be going to the little room on an even day. Patricia Kent arrives at Room A just as Tripp is opening the door to B.

"Lyla Marks has that room," she says.

"I know. She's letting me use it for today."

Patricia gives him a strange look, so he adds: "It's all good" and a smile.

Once he's inside, he pulls his lyrics from his pocket, sets them on the music stand, and gets out the guitar. Scratched into the back near the top are two words: *Just sing.*

He laughs. Lyla Marks snuck in before orchestra and defaced school property. For him.

He sings and plays, and he even likes the way it sounds.

Woke up today, saw my face in the mirror.
Eyes don't lie, message is clear.
I can hear it. I can see it. I can say it.
I'm odd.

I'm a graph without coordinates, a shape without form,
Always deviating away from the norm.
Logic can't fix what's wrong with me.
I'm odd. I'm odd. I'm odd. Indeed.

I've got superhuman cilia in my ear,
Which gives me the ability to hear the fears
And lies that people hide behind, and what's more,
I can hear which crayon's happy in a box of sixty-four.

I'm a graph without coordinates, a shape without form,
Always deviating away from the norm.
Logic can't fix what's wrong with me.
I'm odd. I'm odd. I'm odd. Indeed.

But when he turns on the recorder, he can't seem to get a line out without making a mistake. The period ends before he has anything worth saving. He is a failure.

After turning down the main hallway, he sees Lyla with a group of friends walking in his direction. Urgent need for a plan. What if she says hi? What if she doesn't? What if she asks about the recording?

A few feet away, a drinking fountain calls to him. He races over, grateful to have something else to steer toward. The group of girls walks by, and he is just about to breathe and continue on to class, when he hears Lyla's voice. "I'll catch up in a minute!" She steps out of the group and walks over to the fountain. His feet have frozen, but his face is hot. "Excuse me," she says without really looking at him. As he moves aside, she slips a note on top of his notebook and bends over to get a drink. Then she's gone.

He ducks into the nearest bathroom and reads it.

Dear Mr. Odd,
    Okay. I admit it. I snuck by the practice room and listened in at the door again, hoping you'd be singing your song. And you were! Fun song, indeed! I love everything about it. Plus you can sing. I knew it.
    —Ms. Even
    P.S. Teach me some chords or something. I want to learn more.

Tripp looks at himself in the mirror and grins.

To the One Who Spies on Unsuspecting Aardvarks,
    I should be paying attention in

science, but I'd rather write you a letter. You should be ashamed for spying. But thank you for saying you liked my song. When I tried to record it, I choked.

Maybe if you want to learn more about playing guitar, you should start with the 12-bar blues because it's easy and it's the basis of a lot of songs. I learned all about the different blues progressions off the Internet. Once you learn the basic chord progression, you can play it in any key. The easiest key to start with is probably E. So here's a chord progression:

E-E-E-E7
A7-A7-E-E
B7-A7-E-E

-Odd
P.S. Since you gave up the little room today, you can use it tomorrow. Write a blues song. You can mix up the chords, use less, use more, whatever.

When the bell rings, he hurries to Lyla's locker and slips in the note.

Lyla's Room; 7:16 p.m.

<To: Tripp Broody> October 20

Dear Odd,

I would have replied right away, but after school I had to practice. Thanks for the tips and the offer to have the room, but Annie is in Room A on odd days. If she knew we traded days, she'd want me and you to switch so that I'd always have the little room on odd days, and to be honest, I am kind of enjoying a break from Annie. That sounds horrible. I feel guilty about it, but it's true.—Even

<To: Lyla Marks> October 20

Okay, twist my arm. I'll take the little room two days in a row. I'll try to find a way to make it up to you. Stop feeling guilty about everything. It's okay to want a break from Annie.—Odd

<To: Tripp Broody> October 20

Stop feeling guilty? Okay. The next song I write will be "The Guilt Song." I'm like the murderer in "The Tell-Tale Heart"—when I'm feeling guilty or panicky, my heart pounds like that. Boom. Boom.
—Ms. Even

<To: Lyla Marks> October 20

Dear Ms. Even: How fascinating that you can relate to the murderer in "Tell-Tale Heart." If I hear any boom booms coming from the floor in the room, I'll rip up the boards in search of a still-beating heart. I like the idea of "The Guilt Song." Maybe a boom boom beat. I have massive quantities of guilt. I'll write one, too, and we'll see who finishes first. My problem is that I tend to have ideas throughout the day instead of when I sit down to write.—Odd

<To: Tripp Broody> October 20

You need a notebook you can keep in your pocket.—Ms. Even

OCTOBER 21. TUESDAY.

PRACTICE ROOM B; 11:25 A.M.

When Tripp opens the guitar case, there is a pocket-size homemade notebook waiting for him, paper cut to size and stapled at the fold. On the front cover, a sketch of a guitar. On the back: *Brought to you by the Thrum Society*.

He records his "Mr. Odd" song — the whole thing this time without stopping once — and e-mails her the MP3 file. It isn't perfect, but it's done and it feels good. Then he opens the notebook and starts writing song number two. "Guilty." He writes the title in the center of a page and jots down anything and everything that comes to mind, searching for connections and rhymes.

need a
lawyer
trial

get arrested
GET BUSTED
for doing
nothing

lock me up!

feel
guilt

setup!
innocent until
proven guilty

I'm
just
guilty of
being me

(GUILTY)

NOTHING

of crimes? →

lying
cheating
fraud
counterfeit

guilty of
being born

↓

OF THINKING
about a
crime?

thorn
torn
worn

✳ time
doin time?

aggravated
assault

OCTOBER 22. WEDNESDAY.

PRACTICE ROOM B; 11:44 A.M.

Lyla is singing her song again. She doesn't know quite where this voice of hers came from. It's as if there's a creature living inside her that she never realized was there. And now it's coming out in this song.

> *Guilt on my sleeve and the bottom of my shoe.*
> *Guilt under my collar sticks to me like glue.*
> *Swallowed it on Sunday, and it's eatin' me alive.*
> *Buried it on Monday, but it just won't die.*
>
> *'Cause it's beating beating beating*
> *Like a telltale heart.*
> *Can't make it stop once it starts . . .*

When she's done, she glances up. A small notebook of her own has been slipped under the door. She picks it up. The first page has a note:

Ms. Even,

I was going to slip this blank notebook under the door, but I couldn't help stopping to listen to your new song. So then I decided to write you a note in it first. Your song rocks. I know you can't sing too loudly in here, but I could hear all this energy. Are you playing it in E, which is the key I gave you the blues progression for? If so, try a Hendrix chord in place of the E7 when you get to the beating part. I think it would sound cool. Here's the diagram for the chord, which is named after Jimi Hendrix, of course. God of Guitar. I'm going to make you some guitar-playing videos and send you the links.

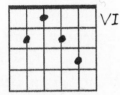

The Roman numeral VI means you play this on the 6th fret

Lyla opens the door. The hallway is empty.

OCTOBER 23. THURSDAY.

PRACTICE ROOM B; 11:37 A.M.

"Hello." Tripp looks into the camera and freezes. He stops and resets it so that the camera is focused only on his hands, not on his face. He starts again. "Here's my tip of the day. One way to get a cool percussive sound out of your strum is to stop the strings from vibrating with your palm. Try strumming once, then instead of strumming again, just thump your right hand down on the strings, then strum again normally. Experiment with the rhythm. . . ."

He demonstrates and moves on to another tip. Before the period is over, he uploads four tip files, posts them on YouTube, and sends Lyla the links.

OCTOBER 24. FRIDAY.

ROCKLAND HALLWAY; 3:16 P.M.

Lyla pulls the notebook Tripp gave her from her pocket and rereads the lyrics for her guilt song, wishing that she could slip through the laws of time and space and float in a bubble of invisibility. If she could, she'd spend as much time as she wanted writing songs. Instead, she is supposed to meet Annie by her locker and go shopping with her mom to pick out new performance outfits.

Her phone buzzes. Annie. Reluctantly, Lyla puts away the notebook, closes her locker, and answers as she starts walking.

"Hey, Annie—I'm just leaving my locker now and—"

"Why didn't you tell me first?" Annie's voice is clipped with anger.

"What?"

"The talent show. If you wanted to do a solo, you should've told me first. And since when do you play the guitar?"

Lyla's heart pounds. "I don't know what you're talking about. Where are you?"

Annie hangs up.

Confused, Lyla changes direction and heads toward the music wing. The sign-up sheet for the talent show is posted in the hallway outside the orchestra room. In Tripp's handwriting, her name is written in the 4:30 audition slot: *Lyla Marks guitar and vocal solo.*

The orchestra room door opens and Annie walks out.

"Annie! Tripp wrote that. It's a joke. Look, I'm crossing it off."

"Tripp?"

"We were talking about the talent show, and he was joking about how I should play the guitar instead of the cello, and then he must've written that."

Annie glares, turns without a word, and begins walking down the hall toward the front entrance.

Lyla follows. "Don't be mad."

Annie keeps walking.

"Come on, Annie. Stop."

Annie stops, pressing her lips together, her eyes darkening. "I asked you the other day what's going on between you and Tripp, and you said nothing."

"We had a conversation. Do I have to report every single conversation I have with anybody?"

"I'm not mad, Lyla," Annie says quickly. "I just know he's not right for you. He's abnormal, Lyla. He doesn't have any friends and — "

"Annie, you're talking about him like he's a boyfriend. He's not. Forget it. Look, I'm not doing a solo. It was a joke."

They stand looking at each other awkwardly. Then Annie looks at the place on the sign-up sheet where Lyla had crossed out what Tripp had written. "You're not going to do a solo?"

"No."

"Do you still want to go shopping?" Annie asks.

Lyla winces internally and tries not to show it.

"Now what?" Annie's eyebrows raise. "You can't go?"

Annie gives her an opening, and a lie comes spilling out. "I want to, Annie. But my dad called and said that I have a dentist appointment. But we can go this weekend!"

"Whatever you say, Lyla." Annie walks away.

"Don't be mad at me!" Lyla adds. "Be mad at my dad. Or the dentist. Or my teeth."

Annie disappears, and the hallway is quiet. She feels guilty but also relieved. A long walk home sounds just right. She waits until she's sure Annie is gone, and then heads out. In front of the school, the maple tree is blazing red against the brilliant blue sky. Every leaf seems to be singing with color. She takes a breath and starts walking.

Her phone buzzes, and she is happy to see Tripp's name. "You got me in trouble with Annie," she says. "The guitar solo sign-up thing . . ."

"I didn't think about that. Sorry."

"Yeah. I'll get you back."

"Are you threatening me with revenge of some sort, Ms. Even?"

"I'm signing you up for the talent show audition. Four twenty time slot. Don't be late."

"Villain! Erase it."

"What good is playing music if you don't share it?"

"Music doesn't have to be shared to be worthwhile."

"Yes, it does." She crosses the street. "Otherwise it's like one hand clapping."

"If I'm alone in the forest and I sing a song, isn't that good for my soul? Isn't that worth something?"

She laughs. "Okay. True. I sing in the shower."

"Aha!"

"But music is better if it's shared."

"Have you ever sung in public?"

"No."

"Why not?"

"I play the cello. That's what I do."

"*Bawk.*"

"I'm not the chicken. I'm auditioning for the talent show with Annie."

"Okay. I will admit it. I'm a chicken. Erase me."

"The truth comes out."

"Did you erase me?"

"I never wrote you in."

He laughs. "Good. Well, I hope the rest of your day is . . . odd."

She laughs. "Oooh. Well, in that case, I hope the rest of your day is nice and even. Bye."

"Adios."

She closes her phone.

Lining the street is a row of old oak trees, each one holding up its chorus of crimson and gold leaves. Lyla looks up and smiles as a cool breeze rustles her hair.

Whenever she's with Annie, she feels tense, but when she talks with Tripp, something nice happens inside her: a vibration, a thrum. It's as if a tiny wind chime is suspended inside her soul, she thinks, and his words are the wind that makes it ring.

OCTOBER 25. SATURDAY.

Tripp's Room; 1:23 p.m.

<u>Guilty</u>

Cheating and lying   + *conniving*
Fraud and forgery
Aggravated screaming
Dreaming of conspiracy
Flawed in every ~~way~~   *thought*
I'm a twisted guarantee
I'm a menace I'm a thorn
I should never have been born

Oh

I'm guilty... I'm guilty ←
Doin' time for my crime

Do this
3 times

War

~~All kinds~~ of crimes
Won't deny 'em

2

~~I'm~~ busted
Tried without a trial
No lawyer by my side
~~I think I'm gonna die~~

I'm hanging
out to dry

I'm guilty... I'm guilty
Doin' time for my crime

x3
guitar solo
here

OCTOBER 26. SUNDAY.

Practice Room B; 11:39 a.m.

Tripp is playing in the little room when his cell phone buzzes. He brightens when Lyla's name appears.

"Hey," he says. "It's against the rules to use cell phones during the school day. Where are you?"

"In the girls' bathroom." Lyla giggles. "I'm calling because I've got a dare for you."

"If it has anything to do with the girls' bathroom, I'm not doing it."

"Tomorrow at lunch . . . come to Room B."

"But it's an even day."

"That's the point. I'll let you in. And then we'll play each other the songs we've been working on. I finally figured out the chorus for my Hendrix-chord guilt song."

"What about Jacoby's rule? There can't be more than one person using a room at the same time."

"You make it sound like a law of physics. Jacoby's Rule: If Mr. Odd and Ms. Even are ever in the same room at the same time, they will cancel each other out in total annihilation, like when matter and antimatter collide."

"You're blowing my mind. First, I never thought Lyla Marks would break a rule, and second, you sound like a science geek."

"I love physics. Force equals Mass times Acceleration."

"Okay. Maybe I'll accelerate my mass to the little room tomorrow."

Lyla laughs, and the sound makes him happy.

OCTOBER 28. TUESDAY.

PRACTICE ROOM B; 11:31 A.M.

Tripp is almost at the door to Practice Room B when he loses his nerve and turns around. He is heading back to the orchestra room when he hears Patricia Kent's voice in the hallway ahead. She is coming this way. He turns back and quickly knocks on Room B's door.

The door opens and he slips in.

Lyla is wearing blue jeans, a soft green T-shirt, and a scarf with lots of fringe. Her brown eyes have this intense warmth, as if they have some superhuman power to mend broken bones or unlock doors, he thinks.

"You made it!" she whispers.

The guitar is out, propped against the bench, like an old friend. He relaxes a bit.

"Did Jacoby see you?" she asks.

"No," he whispers back.

They listen to the sound of Patricia approaching. Her door closes.

Lyla puts her finger to her lips. "Wait 'til she starts playing," she says.

After a minute, the French horn begins.

Lyla holds up her lunch. "I'm eating tuna fish," she says.

"No pomegranate?" he asks.

"Just tuna."

He nods. "I can smell."

"Sorry," she says. "I'll open a window."

"Yes, please," he says. "The one with the ocean view."

She laughs.

"I'm just realizing this room is the size of a Pop-Tarts box," he says.

"Tuna fish–flavored Pop-Tarts. Sorry."

"This is momentous," he says.

"The smell?"

"No. Being in the same room at the same time . . . I'm nervous."

Lyla smiles. "*That's* what is so different about you."

"That I'm nervous?"

"That you admit it. Most people don't say that kind of thing out loud. Most people pretend they're not nervous about stuff like this."

"What does that make me?"

Her eyebrows raise. "Odd?" She is about to add that she is nervous, too. But he has crouched to look at the cello lying sideways on the floor.

"Play me some Mozart-arello on the cello," he says.

"No. Play me your new song on the guitar." She picks it up and hands it to him.

He sits on the floor and strums a chord, then sings. *"Home, home on the range, where the deer and the antelope play . . ."*

She laughs.

"Okay. Let your song rip." He holds out the guitar to her.

"I'm too nervous. It's easier to play my cello in front of a million people than it is to play one guitar chord in front of you."

"I won't look."

"I'll only do my song if you do yours," she says.

"Okay, but you go first."

She takes out the notebook he had given her and opens it up so that she can look at the lyrics if she starts to forget.

"Nice notebook," he says.

She smiles and he turns so that his back is to her. The wall is absolutely blank.

She plays and sings, her voice sliding into the room, picking up confidence and strength as she goes.

Guilt on my sleeve and the bottom of my shoe.
Guilt under my collar, sticks to me like glue.
Swallowed it on Sunday, and it's eatin' me alive.
Buried it on Monday, but it just won't die.

And it's beating beating beating like a telltale heart,
Beating beating beating like a telltale heart,
Beating beating beating like a telltale heart.
Can't make it stop once it starts.

Guilt on my tongue leaves a bitter taste.
Guilt in my bloodstream, running through my veins.
Hide it on Tuesday, but I got no choice.
Friday rolls around and you can hear it in my voice.

'Cause it's beating beating beating like a telltale heart,
Beating beating beating like a telltale heart,
Beating beating beating like a telltale heart.
Can't make it stop once it starts.

Don't tell me you can't hear it when I walk into the room,
Louder every minute, going boom boom boom.

When she gets to the final chorus, her voice opens up
and envelops him.

Beating beating beating like a telltale heart,
Beating beating beating like a telltale heart,

Beating beating beating like a telltale heart.
Can't make it stop once it starts.

She finishes and there is silence. "You didn't like it?"

He turns around. "It was amazing. Really. I'm stunned."

Lyla smiles. "Yeah?"

"Where did that come from? It's so . . . not Bach."

She laughs. "I know. A month ago, if you would've told me that I'd write a song like this, I'd say you were crazy. I used to think that, in order to write a song, I'd have to hear it in my head, and then I'd sit down with a pen and write it out in notation. That's the way you see Mozart and Beethoven doing it in movies about them. But your way, of just playing until you find something by accident, makes a lot more sense. It's like every song is a series of accidents."

"Your song is a really good accident."

His smile makes her smile.

"Well, anyway," she says, "I'm not sure how to end the song."

He takes the guitar. "Maybe go back to the Hendrix E chord and punch up the rhythm?" He tries it and teaches her a new strumming rhythm and her eyes light up. She takes the guitar back and practices.

"That's great." He watches her. "I can't believe how fast you learn."

"All that cello," she says. "Let me borrow your pick."

Tripp hesitates.

"I'm not going to steal it," she says.

"It's . . ."

"Ssh!" She whispers. "I thought I heard Jacoby's voice."

"His rule is stupid."

"He's afraid if there are two people in here, we'll talk instead of play."

"Two students talking to each other. Call the police."

Lyla listens until she's sure the teacher isn't there. "Okay. It's your turn." She hands him the guitar and turns to face the wall. "No wailing or we'll get kicked out."

"I'm not going to sing."

"*Bawk.*"

"My lyrics aren't great." He pulls out the notebook that she'd given him.

"Nice notebook," she says, and smiles.

He opens it to his lyrics page and reads over his notes. "What's interesting is that we both wrote in the key of E." He plays a chord.

She smiles. "We're on the same wavelength. Come on, sing."

He's nervous, but he sings.

> *Cheating, lying, and conniving,*
> *Fraud and forgery,*
> *Aggravated screaming,*
> *Dreaming of conspiracy,*
> *Flawed in every thought,*
> *I'm a twisted guarantee,*

I'm a menace, I'm a thorn.
I should never have been born.

I'm guilty, oh guilty,
I'm guilty, oh guilty,
I'm guilty, oh guilty,
Doin' time for my crime. Boom Boom Boom.

War crimes, won't deny 'em,
Busted, tried without a trial,
No lawyer by my side,
I'm just hanging out to dry.
I'm a menace, I'm a thorn.
I should never have been born.

I'm guilty, oh guilty,
I'm guilty, oh guilty,
I'm guilty, oh guilty,
Doin' time for my crime. Boom Boom Boom.

When he's done, she leaps to her feet. "I think they're polyphonic!"

"Polyphonic?"

"Two different melodies that fit together! Lots of baroque music is polyphonic. Bach was all over it. This is so cool. Let's record both our songs and play them at the same time and see if they fit."

They record Lyla's song first and then Tripp's at the

same tempo. Then, they layer them in the same file and play them back. Each phrase neatly overlaps the other, their voices fitting together in harmony.

Lyla's eyes sparkle. "The opposite of annihilation!"

Tripp laughs. "Indeed."

Rockland Hallway; 3:16 p.m.

As Lyla walks down the hall, she pulls out her cell phone and calls Tripp.

"Howdy," he answers.

She presses the phone against her ear so she can hear him over the hallway noise. "Hey, do you have Sanders for science?" she asks.

"No. I have Peakly."

"Are you on chapter three? Didn't you think it was interesting? The whole eardrum thing." There is a tap on her shoulder. She turns—it's Tripp—and she almost screams.

"Sorry!" He laughs.

She looks around for Annie. "It's just—"

"You don't want anybody to see you talking to me?"

"No! It's not that. It's just Annie. She'd make a huge deal out of it. She wouldn't leave it alone."

"Well, some people make a big deal about everything. Anyway, you're lucky you have Sanders for science. Peakly's voice is so annoying. I try to block it out."

"But the sound unit is so interesting! My voice is

literally playing a tiny little teeny drum in your ear."

"What?"

"How sound works. Right now, I'm talking and the sound is coming out of me as a wave of air, each air molecule pushing on the next until it travels all the way to your ear. When the wave reaches your eardrum, your eardrum vibrates, and that's how the sound gets in you. So my voice is literally playing a little drum in your ear. Tell me that's not cool."

"You really are a geek. And it's cool."

Lyla spots Annie down the hall. "You have to go."

"I do?"

"Annie's coming."

"Okay, science guru."

He leaves and she rushes over to her locker and makes herself busy, pretending to text.

"So," Annie says. "Who are you texting?"

"My dad." Lyla puts away her phone and crouches down to pull her French book from the stack on the bottom. "I was just reminding him that we're staying for Sweet Tooth."

"What's this?" Annie pulls the notebook Tripp gave her out of Lyla's back pocket.

Lyla stands up and grabs it back. "Nothing."

"Wow!" Annie says. "Somebody's touchy."

Lyla sees the suspicion in Annie's face, but she smiles as if nothing is wrong.

OCTOBER 29. WEDNESDAY.

Practice Room B; 11:25 a.m.

The room is empty without Lyla. Tripp misses her immediately. He opens the guitar case and finds a note.

Dear Mr. Odd,
    Since you are inspiring me to write songs that I never thought I'd write, it's my turn to inspire you. Your assignment is to write a waltz. ¾ time. That means the beat of the song is
    1, 2, 3,
    1, 2, 3,
    1, 2, 3,

Get it?
—Ms. Even

He gets it. A challenge. A dare.

ROCKLAND HALLWAY, 3:13 P.M.

Lyla sees Tripp in the crowded hallway, and her face breaks into a smile. She starts looking for Annie and then catches herself because she remembers that Annie said she had to leave early today for an orthodontist appointment.

"Howdy, Mr. Odd," she says. "You look positively chipper."

He laughs. "I am! Because of what you told me yesterday about the physics unit, I actually paid attention, and guess what."

"You learned something?"

"You're going to hear about it when you have science tomorrow. It's cool." His eyes get bigger. "It validates my Vibe Theory."

"What's that?"

"Remember when I told you that I've always felt like I could feel the vibes of inanimate objects?"

She nods and laughs. "You can hear which crayon in the box is happy."

"Exactly. Well, Peakly said that everything vibrates."

160

"Even dead things?"

"Everything. Even dead things. Even pomegranates. This pencil, even though it's perfectly still, is vibrating because all matter is made up of molecules, and all molecules are made of atoms, and all atoms vibrate all the time." He holds the pencil to her ear. "Can you hear it?"

"No."

"Well, that's your problem."

"I thought I had a problem," she says. "I just never knew what it was."

Tripp smiles. "Every vibration is a sound; therefore everything has a sound."

"Therefore you can hear the pencil?"

"We can't hear the pencil because it's vibrating at a rate we can't detect, but it's making a sound."

"Like the dog whistle thing!" she says.

"Exactly."

"So if I had the eardrums of a dog, maybe I could actually hear my bones grow!"

He grins.

She goes on. "The other day, I walked out and saw the maple tree, you know, the one in front? And the leaves were so red, I had this feeling that they were actually singing."

"I'm not the only odd one."

She grabs his pencil and tucks it behind her ear. "Now we're both physics geeks."

"I'm also chipper because I'm writing a song," he says.

"Hmmm, let me use my superhuman cilia and listen to your thoughts." She closes her eyes as if she is in a trance. "Could it be . . . are you writing a waltz?"

"Yep. I decided to call it 'The Pomegranate Waltz.'"

"I want to hear it."

"I can hear the melody for the verses and the chorus, but I haven't come up with any lyrics yet."

They reach her locker and she stops. "We could work on it together in the little room on Thursday," she says.

"A collaboration," he says. "Batman and Robin."

"Bonnie and Clyde."

"Bert and Ernie."

"Jekyll and Hyde."

"Shouldn't we be naming musicians?" he asks.

She laughs.

THE METRO; 4:09 P.M.

As soon as Tripp sits down on the Metro train, his phone buzzes, and he almost groans out loud when he sees that it's his mom calling.

"Tripp! I want to talk with you about something." Her voice has that forced cheerful buzz. "I think it's something you'll like. I've made an appointment with an advisor at Crenshaw—"

BOOM! The walls cave in. "You have got to be

kidding," he says. "I'm not going to change schools." The doors shut and the train pulls out. "Tell me that you've made an appointment because they need new carpeting."

"I've been thinking that it might be a good place for you. Small class sizes. Top-notch teachers."

"Making me go to a tutor session is one thing. But you cannot make me go to a new school."

"You're not getting anywhere at Rockland and—"

"I'm actually starting to like science, Mom." The train rumbles around a curve.

"You didn't turn in your algebra homework. I saw the zero on Edline this morning."

"I'll get my grades up."

"Which is what you said during the entire second semester last year, and it didn't happen. Anyway, I made an appointment—"

"—which you will cancel," Tripp says.

"—for tomorrow at five thirty."

"No."

"Hear me out." Her voice sweetens. "It's just a preliminary interview. If you come with me to Crenshaw and behave yourself during the interview and genuinely have an open mind about listening to what it might offer you, then I will let you have your guitar back."

The earth screeches to a stop in its orbit.

"You will let me have my guitar back?" he asks.

"Yes."

"When?"

"Right after the interview. We'll drive straight to the store and get it."

"Seriously?"

"Seriously."

"It's a deal." He agrees, hangs up, and immediately calls Lyla.

She answers in a whisper. "Hello, Mr. Odd."

"Why are you whispering?" he asks.

"I'm in my private lesson with Dr. Prevski, but she just went to the bathroom."

"I'm getting my guitar back tomorrow."

"Hurray!" she whispers. "That's great."

"Thanks. I'll let you go. Adios."

"Au revoir."

"Ta-ta. That's good-bye in Thai."

"Is not. Cheerio. That's good-bye in Old English."

"May the force be with you."

"That's what science geeks say."

"Takes one to know one." He gets off the train and sees a musician playing. "Lyla, wait! Listen . . ." He holds out his phone so that she can hear the sound of the echoing trumpet. "I'm in the Metro. Somebody's playing."

"We should do that," Lyla says. "Got to go."

He closes his phone and stands still. It's an old jazz song that he has heard before. His favorite elementary school teacher used to sing it all the time. "What a Wonderful World." The trumpet's soaring voice rides into the air. Tripp imagines each note causing a ripple effect in the air, sending wave after wave of sound into his ears. He imagines the sound playing his tiny eardrums and the vibration of the drum sending the waves of sound through his entire body, striking against the strings of his soul.

The musician catches him watching, and they share a wordless nod of appreciation, musician to musician, while the song goes on.

LYLA'S HOUSE; 9:42 P.M.

Lyla is dishing up bowls of ice cream for herself and her dad when her phone rings. It's on the table closest to him, so he picks it up and looks at the display.

"Who is Tripp and why is she calling so late?"

Lyla jumps over to the table and takes the phone. "Oh . . . it's a he. I mean, he's a him. He's probably calling about homework. He's in my algebra class." She answers, pressing the phone into her ear. "Hi."

"So, if everything has a sound," Tripp says, "then the moon must have a sound."

Lyla glances at her dad. "Hold on, Tripp. Let me get my backpack. I can read you the assignment."

Tripp laughs. "Wow, Ms. Even. Is that the first time you've ever called me by my actual name?"

"Why can't he check Edline?" her dad asks.

"Does this mean I have to call you Lyla?" Tripp asks.

"Hold on." Lyla lowers the phone. "Dad, it's not a big deal. He's just missing the algebra assignment." Before her dad can say another word, she grabs her backpack and takes it into her bedroom. "Okay, I'm back," she says into the phone.

"I *am* missing the algebra assignment, but that's not why I called," Tripp says.

Lyla throws her backpack on her bed and closes her door. "I didn't want to have to explain anything to my dad."

"Sorry. I called at a bad time."

"No, it's okay. I'm in my room now."

"So the question is: what sound do you think the moon makes?"

Lyla walks over to the window. The overhead light in her room throws a superimposed image of her reflection on the glass. She presses her face to the window, cupping her hand around her eyes to block out the light. The crescent moon's whiteness is brilliant and wild, as if its source of light is coming from its own state of mind.

"I think it's wailing," Tripp says, and he starts singing this funny falsetto.

Lyla's dad opens her door, and Lyla turns to her desk and picks up a pencil. "You're supposed to do problems one through six. Got it?"

"You turned into a mean algebra machine," Tripp says. "Why can't you say, 'Excuse me, Dad, but I'm trying to listen to the moon'?"

She walks over to her backpack on the bed and puts the pencil in the side pocket. "I can't really give you the answers, Tripp. You have to figure out the solutions yourself."

"Hurt me, Ms. Even," Tripp says.

Her dad's presence in the room is like a black hole, pulling her in when she'd rather be talking with Mr. Odd. Reluctantly, she says good-bye. As she closes the phone, her dad hands her the bowl of ice cream.

"It seems rude of this Tripp to call and expect you to give him the answers."

She turns her back so that that he can't see her smile. She likes the sound of Tripp's name in the room, even if her dad has no idea who he is. "He's not rude," she says, glancing out the window. "Just . . . well . . . odd."

OCTOBER 30. THURSDAY.

PRACTICE ROOM B; 11:33 A.M.

Tripp knocks on the practice room door and it opens. "Mr. Odd!"

Tripp steps in and smiles. He remembers a report he wrote in the sixth grade about how monarch butterflies migrate from the north every year to the same fir trees thousands of miles away in Mexico and imagines that stepping into this room feels as good to him as landing on a Mexican fir tree must feel to a migrating butterfly.

"Let's hear your 'Pomegranate Waltz'!" She hands him the guitar and sits on the bench.

He sits on the floor and tunes up. "This was a hard assignment. I've never written anything in three/four time. I kind of like my tune, but you need to help me think of lyrics." He plays and hums the melody.

"Ooooh, it's actually pretty," she says.

He winces. "I wrote a pretty song."

"You did. You should be proud of that. A great musician can write all kinds of songs."

He keeps playing, and when he comes around to the verse again, she sings, "*I like the sound of a pomegranate. I must be from another planet.*" She laughs.

"*My planet is mostly made of granite,*" he sings, and stops. "See? It's impossible."

"It doesn't have to have the word *pomegranate* in it," Lyla says. "Play it again. I'll sing the first thing that comes to my mind."

He plays.

She sings, "*I like the sound of your name in my ear.*" She stops and blushes. "I didn't mean *you* you. I mean it doesn't have to be based on anything true, right? We can make up a song, imagining someone is singing it about someone else. Forget it. Let's start over."

"No. It's a good first line. Let's keep going. *I like the sound of your name in my ear. I like to hear . . .*"

"*What you have to say?*"

"That's good. Then something that rhymes with *say* . . . *I want to pay you lots of money . . .*" He sings and laughs.

"How about *I'd like to pay attention to you?*"

"*. . . instead of doing my homework.*"

"*Instead of doing all the things I have to do.*"

"Good. Good. But let's make it shorter. *Instead of doing what I have to do.*"

Lyla writes their lyrics in her notebook. "Okay, let's sing what we have so far."

> *I like the sound of your name in my ear.*
> *I like to hear what you have to say.*
> *I'd like to pay attention to you—instead of doing*
> *What I have to do.*

"Ooh," she says. "It sounds good. Sing it again and I'll try singing harmony."

"I don't know if I can sing if you're doing that."

"Yeah, you can. Sing your note and hold on to it no matter what I sing. You have to listen to yourself and don't let yourself be pulled off the note. Imagine you're on one street and I'm on the other. Parallel. We're going in the same direction, but you have to stay in your lane."

"Okay."

"Sing this note." She gives him a note. He sings it. "Now stay there." She adds her note one third above it.

She makes him practice it a few times, and he gets it.

"We're good," she says.

"Actually really good!" he admits. "We should play in the Metro."

"You need a permit," Lyla says. "I read an article about it once. You have to send in an audition video."

"Well, we should do it. Or we should do weddings. I

was at this wedding in September and the music was really bad. We could do a lot better."

"We could!"

Without warning, the door opens and Ms. Kettering and Mr. Jacoby are staring at them.

"Lyla!" Mr. Jacoby says.

Lyla jumps up. "We were just working on some music together."

"I know I made the rules perfectly clear," Mr. Jacoby says. "Practice rooms are not for socializing."

"We're not socializing," Tripp says. "We're—"

"Save your explanation," Ms. Kettering says. "Come up to the resource room. I'd like to talk with you and Benjamin."

As Tripp puts away the guitar, Mr. Jacoby explains that he has lost privileges to use the practice room. Period.

Lyla blanches. "But it was my idea. I'm the one who should lose privileges."

Tripp protests, but Ms. Kettering hustles him out the door.

ROCKLAND HALLWAY; 3:16 P.M.

Lyla has walked through the afternoon in shock, unable to concentrate on anything except the thought of Tripp not being allowed back into the practice room. The effort it has taken to get through each class, to pretend that nothing is wrong, has made her feel sick to her stomach. As soon as her last class ends, she texts Annie to say that she doesn't need a ride home today. It's another lie, but she needs to find Tripp.

She hurries to her locker, and just as she is about to send him a text, Annie arrives.

"Hey, Lyla, I heard something interesting about Tripp Broody today." Although Annie's voice is light, Lyla can hear a current of hostility running through it.

"Really?" Heat rushes to Lyla's face. She focuses on her backpack, pretending to struggle with the zipper.

Annie goes on. "It was my day to tutor and I was in the resource room, and Ms. Kettering found out that Tripp has been skipping tutoring sessions with Benjamin Fick."

Lyla stuffs a notebook in her backpack and zips it up. "How did she find that out?" She tries to sound casual and starts walking.

Annie follows. "I'm not sure, but anyway, I was talking to Patricia Kent, and she said that Tripp was playing guitar in one of the practice rooms, which doesn't make any sense because you're in there. Did you see him? I mean, you were there today, right?"

Lyla's heart pounds. "I don't know anything about it."

Annie stops and glares. "That was a test, Lyla. And you failed. You've been lying, and I'm so sick of it. You promised that you weren't going to hang out with him, and so what do you do? You go behind my back." She speeds ahead.

"I wasn't trying to deliberately go behind your back, Annie. You don't understand." Lyla catches up.

"I do understand. I talked to Patricia Kent. She said you never even asked her to trade days. She said she heard you in the practice room with him."

"Did you tell on us to Ms. Kettering?"

"I'm sure she figured it out on her own."

"I don't believe you."

Annie stops and shrugs. "Well, that's too bad."

"Look, Annie. I'm sorry I lied. But I . . . I was . . . I've been feeling like . . ."

"Like you want to dump me—"

"Stop it, Annie."

"No, you stop it, Lyla."

"I don't think there's a law that says we have to do everything together all the time."

"That's what friends do, Lyla."

"But you put this pressure on me, like I can't ever disagree."

"Just say it, Lyla. You hate me. You think you're better than me."

"Stop it! I don't think I'm better than you. I don't hate you! You're the one who is always saying 'I hate you' to me. How do you think that makes me feel?"

Annie's face hardens. "So what do you and Tripp do in the practice room?"

"We play the guitar."

An ugly laugh flies out of Annie.

Lyla asks, "Why is that funny?"

"It's so not you." She walks on. "Have a great life, Lyla."

THE BROODYS' CAR; 4:27 P.M.

Tripp says nothing to his mom when she picks him up. Now that he has been kicked out of the practice room, the stakes are higher. He has to get his guitar back. Ms. Kettering said she would contact his mom. Maybe she left a message on the home phone and his mom hasn't had a chance to check the messages. Thankfully, he sees no sign of distress in her face. On the way to Crenshaw, she chatters away, reminding him of all the things he can do to make a good impression: eye contact, firm handshake, no mumbling, and definitely no sarcasm. "Act curious about something they mention," she says, "and nod to show you're interested even if you're not."

"Dishonesty above all," Tripp can't resist saying.

She throws him a look. "You know what I mean."

They drive into the city and turn into a wealthy-looking neighborhood. At the end of the street, the school sits on top of a hill, like an old English mansion, ivy growing up the stone walls, a clock tower in the biggest building. Tripp is led into a room with two round-faced people for a "getting to know you" session while his mom has a conference with the financial aid advisor in another room.

When he comes out, the interviewers are smiling, Tripp is smiling, Tripp's mother is smiling, the secretary who says good-bye to them on the way out is smiling.

"I avoided sarcasm, whipped out some impressive vocab, and managed a straight face even though they looked like Tweedledee and Tweedledum," he says as they walk down the steps toward the parking lot. "So . . . now we get the guitar?"

His mom waits until they pass by two women talking next to a red convertible. Then her smile dissolves and her voice darkens. "I'll tell you when we get in the car."

His stomach drops. She gets in the car and slams the door, and he stands there wondering how long it would take him to walk home. She reaches over and opens the door. As he gets in, she explodes. "I can't believe you've been lying to me." She grips the steering wheel with her left hand, turns on the engine, and yanks the car into gear. When she turns to see if it's safe to back out, her eyes take a swipe at him. "If Crenshaw lets you in, you're going. That's it. If you get good grades there, then you can have your guitar back for the summer."

"What?"

She pulls out of the Crenshaw entrance, passing through the two black doors of the imposing wrought-iron gate. "There will be no discussion."

His fury builds, but he says nothing. They ride in silence. She drops him off at home and tells him flatly that she is going to pick up some groceries.

The minute he is alone in the house, he lets out a primal scream. Shaking, he walks into his own room and calls Lyla. *Please answer.* She does, and her voice is like a lifeline he grabs to keep from drowning. Right away she can tell that something is wrong.

He crawls into bed and tells her what happened.

"Crenshaw!" she exclaims. "You can't go to Crenshaw."

"I know."

"Did she find out about the practice room?"

"Yeah."

"This is so bad. Annie did, too. We had a huge fight. I really hope—" Her voice changes, and he can tell her father must be there. "It's page seventy-three. We're supposed to find solutions to all the odd numbers."

"I think my solution involves smashing something with a crowbar," he says.

She laughs. "I don't think that will work. See you tomorrow."

Reluctantly, he says good-bye.

TRIPP'S ROOM; 8:26 P.M.

Lyla calls. Her voice is a whisper. "You know what I did to take my mind off everything?"

"Smashed something?"

She laughs. "No. I made us a website and posted our

MP3s on it and said we're available for weddings!" She laughs again. "Check it out. I sent you the URL. And I have a plan. Tomorrow night, meet me at the corner of Sycamore and Twelfth."

"Why?"

"Not telling. Let's make it seven P.M. Don't meander."

"Am I going to like it?"

"Yes. I have to go." She's gone.

He gets his laptop, brings it back to his bed, and fires it up. He finds her e-mail with the URL and clicks on it: www.thrumsociety.com. The website pops up and immediately takes his breath away. Their songs are all there. The Thrum Society. Everything is somehow going to be okay.

Lyla's Room; 9:32 P.M.

Annie/I joined canticle quartet now it's a quintet. Tomorrow cross our names off audition sheet.

Lyla reads the message and a wave of relief washes over her. She doesn't have to be responsible for Annie. It's better this way.

Lyla/I think that's a great idea. Good luck. I'm sure you'll make it.

OCTOBER 31. FRIDAY.

Lyla's Neighborhood; 7:01 p.m.

Tripp arrives at the corner of Sycamore and Twelfth on his bike and looks for Lyla. Kids in Halloween costumes run across the lawn of a small brick apartment building. Lyla is nowhere in sight. His phone rings.

"Where are you?" Lyla asks.

Her voice in his ear is the first real pleasure of the day. "On the corner of Sycamore and Twelfth. Where are you?"

"Elm and Twelfth. How did you get there?"

"Bike."

"Okay. Walk your bike so you don't get ahead of me. Stay on Sycamore and cross Twelfth, heading toward Thirteenth."

"Okay. I'm walking. Where are we going?"

The neighborhood is old, canopied with huge trees. The small apartments give way to houses, decorated for Halloween with jack-o'-lanterns on the porches and ghosts hanging from the trees. The streetlights are on. It's already dark, though not completely.

"Your voice sounds so sad," she says. "Don't be sad. You're going to like this. Keep walking up Sycamore."

"Is that where you live?"

"I live on Ash and Tenth. Keep going up Sycamore."

"Am I going to find a pot of gold?"

"Yes."

"I thought a rainbow was supposed to be the thing that you follow to get a pot of gold, not a voice on a cell phone."

"Hey, look to your right."

As Tripp begins to cross Thirteenth Street, he glances over and sees Lyla in the glow of a streetlight, carrying a cello case, heading in the same direction one street over. "Hi, Ms. Even."

"Hi, Mr. Odd. We're parallel," she says.

"Why aren't we walking together?" he asks.

"We're avoiding suspicion," she says.

"Ah. Why do you have your cello?" he asks.

"You'll see."

Tripp stays on Sycamore and heads up the next block. Most of the houses have fences, which makes it impossible to catch another glimpse of Lyla. "Do I keep walking?"

"Yep."

When he approaches Fourteenth Street, he looks to the right. "The suspense is killing me. . . . Wait . . . wait . . . there you are. Hello, yonder cello player."

"Hello, yonder Oddman. I'm glad to hear some fun in your voice. Keep walking straight ahead. Hey, you know what this means?"

"What?"

"If we keep seeing each other when we're crossing, it means we are walking with the same approximate stride. We could use algebra to determine the length of our strides."

"Geek! Do I keep going straight?"

"Turn right on Fifteenth. If the length of our strides remains the same, we should remain one block apart."

Tripp turns right on Fifteenth and sees Lyla one block ahead. "Hey, where are you going?"

"Left on Walnut."

"You disappeared."

"Ouch."

"What happened?"

"I banged into a garbage can."

Tripp crosses the street and heads down Walnut. "Okay, what do I do on Walnut?"

"Go into the backyard of the house on the corner. The one on the right with lots of trees. I'm already here."

"Am I walking into a trap?"

"Yes, I'm luring you into a dark alley where I intend to rob— What do you have in your pockets?"

"Two dollars and a guitar pick."

"Where I intend to rob you of two dollars and your guitar pick. Hold on. I need both hands for a minute."

"Why?"

"You'll see."

"What about the pot of gold for me? I would like a lot of money so I can buy my own house and my own guitar and live happily ever after."

"Well . . . you might just get your wish."

"You sound like you're out of breath. How come?"

"Just keep walking. You'll see."

Tripp stops. The house on the corner has a tall fence. "You really want me to go into the backyard? Whose house is this?"

"Too many questions. Just come!"

"Do I go through the gate?"

"Yep. I'm already back here. Walk past the house and into the backyard. Bring your bike. All the way in the back. You're going to see a tree house."

"Tree house? What are you, a hobbit? Is your father the Lord of the Rings?"

She laughs. "This isn't my house. It's my neighbor's."

"We're trespassing?"

"Keep walking . . . all the way in the back."

The backyard is deep and dark. In a large oak he sees the faint glow of a tree house. Then the glow brightens, and Lyla peers out of a window, her hair illuminated from behind.

"Wow." He slips his phone into his back pocket.

"Like it?" she calls down.

"Very cool."

"Ready for the next surprise?" she asks.

"I think so."

"Open the cello case," she says. "It's by the trunk."

Tripp sees a dark shape at the base of the tree. He parks his bike, crouches down, and unlocks the case. It takes a few moments for him to figure out what he's seeing inside the case: the school guitar. He laughs.

"I smuggled it out," she says. "I put it in my cello case and left my cello in the practice room. Mr. Jacoby never goes in those rooms. I figured if he did, I'd tell him that I forgot to put it away."

"You stole the school guitar!"

"No," she protests. "Just borrowing until you get your guitar back. I'm merely putting it to good use."

"This is huge. This is monumental. I can't believe you did it."

"It's a crime for a musical instrument to go unplayed. I put the empty guitar case back in the storage closet. Mr. Jacoby won't even know the guitar is gone."

"You're like Robin Hood," Tripp says. "The musical version. You take guitars from the rich and give them to the poor."

Lyla laughs. "Bring it up!"

Tripp slings the guitar around his back and climbs up through the opening in the floor of the tree house.

The candle, which Lyla has set on the only piece of furniture—a small wooden stool—fills the room with a warm, golden glow. The three walls not facing the trunk have windows, complete with wooden shutters. Lyla has opened them all. The floor is lined with thick, striped blankets. The room smells of cedar and wool.

"Wow," Tripp says.

"I used to know Mrs. Victor, the woman who lived here—"

"—in the tree house?"

Lyla smiles. "In the house house. But she died and her kids are all grown up and they can't decide whether to sell it or keep it. They send a gardener once a month, but the house is empty. My secret hideaway." She takes the guitar and strums a chord. "Nobody knows about it."

The sound of the guitar fills the tree house. The moon is framed like a picture in one of the windows. It feels to Tripp as if they have traveled back in time. "I think Mrs. Victor would like that we're here," he says. "It's a crime for a tree house to be uninhabited."

Lyla smiles.

"My idea is to leave the guitar here so that either one of us can come anytime and play. We'll cover it with these blankets to keep it warm at night."

"But that means you won't have it to play at school."

"I know." She shrugs. "But you can't come to the practice room at all, and you really need it."

"You need it, too."

"We both need it, and I figured we could both play it here."

Tripp nods. "Thanks."

"You're welcome. Okay. Let's work on our waltz," Lyla says, and pulls her notebook out. "I wrote the rest of the lyrics. Oh, and guess what else I brought?"

"I can't imagine."

She reaches in her other pocket and pulls out a small digital recorder. "My dad got this for me to record my lessons with Dr. Prevski. We can record our songs up here and post them all on our website."

"You're a genius," he says, and she nods.

They work on the song, and after a few minutes, Lyla's cell phone rings.

"I'm not answering," she says.

They practice different harmonies until they get the song into shape.

"Ready to record it?" Lyla asks.

Tripp nods, and she pushes the button.

He plays the introduction and then they sing:

> I like the sound of your name in my ear,
> I like to hear what you have to say,
> I'd like to pay attention to you—instead of doing
> What I have to do. Oh . . .

Something inside me is ready,
Something inside me is ready,
Something in me's ready—oh,
Here I go . . .

I like the way that our time intertwines.
I want to design each day so we can meet,
Each word a seed that's hoping to grow—no need to hurry,
Let's take it slow. Oh . . .

Something inside me is ready,
Something inside me is ready,
Something in me's ready—oh,
Here I go . . .

I like the shape of the thoughts in your mind.
You've got the kind of edge that I seem to need,
And if you feel the world doesn't care—I'll send a message,
You'll know I'm here. Oh . . .

They sing the chorus one final time and when they get
to the last note, they look at each other and smile.

"Not bad!" Tripp says.

"Oooh, that break you did gave me an idea for something new to try. Maybe for another song," Lyla exclaims
and takes the guitar. "Let me try it with your pick."

He hesitates.

"Just for a minute," she says.

He hands it to her. She strums, but she isn't holding on tightly enough and the pick flies out of her hand. "I'm sorry," she says, her voice bright with embarrassment. She kneels forward, looking for it. "If we can't find it, I'll get you another one."

Tripp looks all around the opening and then heads down the ladder without saying a word. He starts to search the dark, leaf-covered ground.

"I'm sorry!" Lyla says again. "It's not the end of the world, is it? You have other picks, right?" Her phone rings. She doesn't answer it. "Use your cell phone like a flashlight," she suggests.

He opens his phone and crouches down, pointing the light at the leaves around his feet.

"I'll buy you a new pick, Tripp," she calls down.

More silence . . . just the rustle of leaves as he searches through them.

"I'll come back when it's light and look for it tomorrow," she offers.

He keeps looking.

"Are you mad at me?" she asks.

He doesn't say anything.

"This is kind of ridiculous," she says. "It's just a pick."

"It's not just a pick." Tripp kicks the leaves aside and continues to look.

"Fine," she says.

He can hear her covering the guitar with blankets, closing the shutters. When she climbs down the ladder, he moves aside to let her down, and she opens her cell phone to help him look. Her phone buzzes.

"My dad again."

"That's okay. I'll look for it myself," he says.

She answers. "Hi, Dad, I'm on my—" She listens. "No! . . . I'll be home!" Her voice tenses and then snaps. "No! . . . Five minutes. Dad! I'll be home in five minutes." She closes her phone. "This is bad. I should've answered his call right away. When I didn't pick up, he called Annie." She starts to pace. "This is so bad. I told him I was at Annie's, and Annie just said she had no idea where I am. So now they both know I lied."

Tripp keeps looking at the ground, and she explodes. "I'm sorry, but just so you know, I think this whole reaction here is not very nice. Somebody once said to me, 'Why get worked up about something that isn't that important in the big scheme of life?' I mean, it's a little piece of plastic. How much did it cost, like seventy-five cents? Compare that to what it took for me to get this guitar, to get here. And now I'm in trouble."

Tripp doesn't say anything.

She storms off.

Lyla's House; 8:08 p.m.

When Lyla arrives home, her dad is waiting by the door.

"I do not appreciate your lying to me. Where were you?"

Lyla walks in and sets her case down. "Please do not make this into a big deal. I was going to go to Annie's, but then I changed my mind because I haven't been getting along so great with her lately. I should have called and told you. I just wasn't thinking."

"So where did you go?"

"I just walked around for a while."

"With your cello?"

"I went to the park on Walnut and sat for a while," she says.

"Sat for a while? Doing what?"

"Just thinking. Is it against the law to sit and think?"

"I don't like this tone, Lyla."

"I'm sorry. Really, Dad. I'm sorry."

"It's not like you. Why didn't you answer my call?"

"I had the ringer off. I'm sorry, Dad. I don't know what else to say."

"Well, keep the ringer on, Lyla. That's the reason you have a cell phone. So I can reach you."

"Okay. I'm sorry."

"Why did you bring your cello home from school anyway? Dr. Prevski told you that she wants you to practice on your mom's."

"I know. Mr. Jacoby made everybody bring their instruments home for the weekend because the school is cleaning out the storage rooms."

He shakes his head. "I'm very confused by all this. And Annie sounded really upset."

"Annie is always upset, Dad."

The doorbell rings. Trick-or-treaters.

"I'll get it," Lyla says, picking up the bowl of candy. "I'm going to practice in here so I can get the door."

The home phone rings, fortunately, and he goes to answer it.

She hands out the Halloween candy and then rushes to put the empty cello case in her bedroom and to get her mom's cello. In the living room, she sets up a chair and her music stand and is about to start playing when her phone buzzes.

Tripp/I found the pick.

Lyla/I'm so happy for you.

Tripp/I'm sorry. hard to explain.

Lyla/yeah. Gotta go.

Flushed, Lyla puts her phone away and picks up her bow. For the next hour, she plays as a penance for her sins; she plays to reassure her dad that everything is all right; she plays to keep her mind off the worry that she has made some fatal mistake with Tripp; she plays because the house itself seems to demand the music from her.

After a while, there is another knock.

There is Tripp, out of breath, standing in the yellow

glow of their porch light. Before she can react, he puts a letter in the bowl, takes a candy bar, and leaves.

Dear Lyla,

I was upset and maybe I am a psycho, but I want to explain about the pick. It has to do with my dad. My favorite thing to do with him was to go to our place by Little Deer Lake. It's this piece of land in the woods with this lake behind it, and the idea was that we'd build a cabin eventually, but I wasn't strong or big enough to do actual construction, so we did small stuff first. We dug a fire pit and put logs in a circle around it. Then we made wind chimes and hung them up in the trees. Another time, we made a mailbox, which was funny because who would send us mail there? Each time, we'd pitch a tent and light a fire. We'd kayak and take hikes during the day, and at night sit around the campfire and talk about what the cabin would look like.

The last time we went, we found a note in the mailbox. It was a thank-you note from a guy who said he and his friends were hiking and they used our fire pit. He said how much they liked the mailbox and wind chimes, and he left his guitar pick folded up in the note. We thought that was so cool, and I put the pick in my jacket pocket.

It's so strange how you never know what's coming. We went home, and everything was normal. And then that Tuesday, I got called to the office during math class, and my mom was standing there crying. She took me into the parking lot and told me that my dad was in the hospital. He had a brain aneurysm. I wanted to go see him, but she wouldn't let me. That night, I had to stay at home with my aunt, and I just sat there wondering what was going on. Then my mom came home the next day and said he died. I didn't cry. It seemed completely unreal. Then all these relatives came. My dad was Jewish, and Jewish funerals happen really quickly, so the next day, I was at the cemetery, feeling numb, wearing my big jacket over my suit because it was cold. At one point, I stuck my hand in my jacket pocket and when my fingers found the pick, my skin tingled like it had an electric current running through it. Instead of listening to the Rabbi, I kept rubbing my thumb over the pick, thinking about all the times my dad and I spent together at the lake. It gave me something good to focus on. It wasn't until the casket was lowered into the ground that it hit me. The Rabbi handed my mom a shovel, and she started to sob, and then she got ahold of herself, and the sound of the dirt hitting the casket went straight into my chest. It was like—boom. Your dad is really dead. He's not coming back. Ever. I felt the truth of it for the first time, and this huge sadness exploded inside me, and I didn't know how to handle it. I started crying, and I just held on to the pick in my pocket and started talking to my dad in my head. I told him how much I loved him and how much fun we had at the lake and then out of the blue I told him that I was going to get a guitar and learn how to play. A month later, I got one.

I never told anybody about the pick until now. When you dropped it, I thought I was going to die, but I didn't know how to explain all that because I knew you'd feel really badly if it was gone for good.

Now that it's back, safe and sound, I thought I should explain.

Cell phone light was a good idea, Ms. Even. And we wrote a whole song tonight.

—Mr. Odd

TRIPP'S HOUSE; 9:57 P.M.

Lights are glowing in the windows of his house when Tripp rides up the driveway. As he puts his bike in the garage, his phone rings. He sees that it's Lyla calling, and instead of walking in, he sits on the concrete steps to his front door and answers.

"Hi."

"Hi."

"Are you eating Halloween candy?" he asks.

"No. I should. Chocolate is good. Full of antioxidants."

"Why are you whispering?"

"My dad thinks I'm asleep."

"Already?"

"I know. I have MYO and a recital tomorrow. My dad is a big believer in sleep."

"Did you get in trouble?"

"It's okay."

"What about Annie?"

"That's another story. She isn't talking to me."

"I'm sorry." He adds, "I'm really glad you opened the door. I'm kind of afraid of your dad."

Lyla laughs. "How come?"

"I've seen him a couple of times. He looks very . . . intense."

"When have you seen him?"

"Picking you up from school and videotaping at school concerts."

"Yeah. He's intense."

"I was wondering . . . wouldn't he be sad if you went away to Coles?"

"If I get in, he said he's willing to move. He's an accountant, and he can work pretty much anywhere. Hey, thanks for the letter. I'm glad you told me about the pick. I'm sorry I grabbed it, and I'm glad you found it."

"I didn't want you to think I was crazy. I mean, I know you think I'm odd, but I'm not crazy."

"Hey, I uploaded the MP3 of 'The Pomegranate Waltz' to our website. The harmony sounds great."

"Can't wait to hear it."

"I think I hear my dad," Lyla whispers. "I'd better go."

"Do you want to meet at the tree house tomorrow?"

"Can't. I could come on Sunday, though."

"Do you mind if I go by myself tomorrow?"

"That's what it's for."

"Thanks."

"Bye."

Tripp slips into the house and goes straight to his room. He puts on his headphones, calls up their website, and listens to their song. Their voices fit together so perfectly, it makes him, for the first time, actually like the concept of perfection.

NOVEMBER 1. SATURDAY.

TREE HOUSE; 4:31 P.M.

<u>Waiting in a Tree</u>

(Another instant classic by Tripp Broody)

start with finger snaps?

I'm gonna wait out on this limb
All by myself and count my sins
While ants go marching two by two
Looking for you

add breath

Hang on... Hang on...
I'm just waiting for someone to come
Hang on.. Hang on...
Rescue me from what I've done

add Keys

I should go cause you are late
Stuck with the hook, forgot the bait
The seconds crawl, the minutes stall
I'm gonna fall

something here?

try low voice

Hang on... Hang on...
I'm just waiting for someone to come
Hang on... Hang on...
Rescue me from what I have done

——— *"HORNS"* ———

drums harmony

Rock paper scissors and the paper covers rock
I can't win against myself, I'm all out of luck
Rock paper scissors and the paper flies away
Saying: I don't got all day

Hang on... Hang on....
I'm just waiting for someone to come
Hang on... Hang on...
Rescue me from what I have done

HORNS AGAIN

Hang on... Hang on...
Hang on... Hang on...

add horns!

Hang, Hang on...
Hang, Hang on...

add harmony

maybe end with just the beat?

197

NOVEMBER 2. SUNDAY.

TREE HOUSE; 1:31 P.M.

Tripp is in the tree house. He hears the crunch of footsteps first and then Lyla appears below.

"Hark!" He leans out the window, his face flushed and happy. "I brought chocolate and some very juicy news."

"Yeah? Good juicy news or bad juicy news?"

"Sort of good and bad. Come up and I'll tell you."

"How long have you been here?" She starts climbing up.

"Two days. Just kidding. I have been trying to stay as far away from my house as possible. The air in my house is toxic." He picks up the guitar so there is space for her to sit down.

"I need tree air, too," she says. "Yesterday was so hard. Annie and I aren't really talking, but we have to carpool to MYO, so we're sort of just pretending that nothing is wrong when we're around our parents. And at lunch today, my dad was going on and on, planning the Coles audition, and I wanted to tell him that I don't want to go. But I can't. It's really tense." Her face is full of worry. "And then when I was walking over here, I was thinking about how this whole tree house thing isn't going to last. I mean, it's going to get too cold and we're not going to be able to play because our fingers will freeze and your mom will send you to Crenshaw and—"

He stops her. "First of all, we are going to have record high temperatures this fall and winter, so our fingers won't freeze off. Second of all, I'm going to get my grades up so my mom won't send me to Crenshaw. And third of all, you're just going to tell your dad that you don't want to audition for Coles. And—"

"I can't do that."

"Yes, you can. And fourth of all, and here's the good juicy news. . . ." He does a drumroll on top of the guitar. "We have a gig." He smiles.

"What?"

"Listen." He pulls out his phone and calls up his e-mail.

To: trippbroody@sixstrings.com
From: PomegranatePlayers

Date: November 2
Re: wedding

Dear Thrum Society,

We have an Internet alert set up so that every time someone posts an item with the word "pomegranate," we are notified. The MP3 of "The Pomegranate Waltz" is just beautiful. We'd like to book you to play for an upcoming wedding, which will be at our place on Saturday, November 22, at noon. Short notice, I know. Our musician friends who would ordinarily perform are out of the country for the next few weeks, and as soon as we heard your song and saw that you're located only an hour from our place, we thought it was a sign that you should join us. Please let us know if you're interested and how much you charge.

Ruby Darling
The Pomegranate Playhouse
Loblolly, MD
Winner of the Best Regional
Theater Award, NETC

"You wrote that," Lyla says.

"I didn't. I swear. Ruby Darling, whoever that is, wrote it." He hands her the phone so she can see for herself. "The bad news is that we can't do it because it's the day of your Coles audition. Still, I think it is amazing that she wants us."

Lyla reads it again. "I'm going to be really mad at you if this is a joke."

"It's not a joke."

Lyla grins. "Wow."

"Indeed."

"I think we should go for it," she says.

"We can't."

"She says it's an hour from here. The wedding starts at noon. My audition is scheduled at six."

"Isn't your audition in Boston?"

"No. They set up these audition spots all over the country. November twenty-second is the DC audition. I could tell my dad that I have to be somewhere during the afternoon and promise to be back in time." She starts bouncing. "Okay. Okay. Here's the plan. I mean the big plan. First, you're right: we have to get your grades up. I've been thinking . . . there's a physics test and an algebra quiz coming up. So, since you can't play in the little room anymore, let's use our lunchtime to study together. I'll be your Benjamin Fick."

"But then you'd miss out on the little room."

"The guitar isn't there anymore, so I don't need the room. What we need to do is come here so we can practice for the wedding. I was thinking that I could tell my dad that I signed up for something that meets Mondays, Tuesdays, and Fridays after school, and then I could meet you here every Monday, Tuesday, and Friday."

Tripp smiles. "You're a genius."

"Thank you."

"But how would we get to the wedding?"

"We shall take a cab! And we'll be back in time for the audition, so I won't get in trouble."

"Wow. Sounds like a plan."

Lyla smiles. "Let's sing."

TRIPP'S ROOM; 10:01 P.M.

<To: Tripp Broody> November 2

Mr. Odd! I have hatched a brilliant new mini-plan to add to our big plan. I'm supposed to give my cello teacher money for the next four private lessons. But if I tell her I can only do two lessons and keep that money, then we'll have enough to pay for a cab to the wedding and back. How about it? Your partner in crime, Ms. Even

<To: Lyla Marks> November 2

Ms. Even! You are becoming ever more devious. A brilliant plan, indeed, like Bonnie and Clyde. But I've been thinking maybe we're not ready to play in public. —Mr. Odd

<To: Tripp Broody> November 2

Do I hear a bawk? Bawk?

<To: Lyla Marks> November 2

Yes. Yes.

<To: Tripp Broody> November 2

Remember, you are an aardvark, not a chicken.
We're going! Send me Ruby's address so I have it.
Your job is to e-mail Ruby back and say yes.

NOVEMBER 4. TUESDAY.

ROCKLAND HALLWAY; 11:25 A.M.

Tripp/hey, talent show audition today. are you trying out with Annie?

Lyla/nope.

Tripp/you okay with that? I feel bad like I caused it

Lyla/don't feel bad. i didn't want to do it. did you e-mail Ruby?

Tripp/yep.

Lyla/woohoo!

NOVEMBER 5. WEDNESDAY.

CAFETERIA; 11:27 A.M.

"You should like science right now," Lyla says, pulling her sandwich out of her bag. "Forced vibration and resonance."

"Ms. Peakly has a way of turning any material into burned toast," Tripp says, biting into his sandwich.

A table of girls is watching them, and Lyla guesses that they will report what they're seeing to Annie. Lyla doesn't care. She turns her chair so that she can't see them, rummages in her backpack, and pulls out two pencils. She hands one to him. "Okay, let's review what happens when you strike one tuning fork." She taps her pencil against the table and holds it up. "What happened when you did this in class?"

"We didn't do it. Peakly lost control of the class and made us read without talking."

"Well, if I make my tuning fork ring, then the vibrations send a chain reaction through the air all the way to your tuning fork." Lyla makes waves with her fingers moving from her pencil to his. "Then if our tuning forks are identical, yours will ring even if you don't hit it."

"One bell can make another bell ring?"

She nods. "It's called resonance. One object vibrating at the same natural frequency of a second object causes that object to vibrate. That's why we say the phrase 'that resonates' when we agree with something someone says."

He stops eating. "Okay. That matches my Thrum Theory."

"About inanimate objects?"

"No. That's my Vibe Theory." He leans in, blocking out the noise of the cafeteria, and looks at the pencil in her hand. "Here's my Thrum Theory. I think every soul vibrates at a certain frequency," he explains. "It's sort of like each soul has a sound that is its signature—and your soul just wants to feel the vibrations of this sound. I think the vibrations of my soul and the vibrations of the guitar match each other, which is why it feels so right for me to play it."

Lyla's eyes sparkle. "So my vibrations want to connect with vibrations that are in tune with me? And when something feels really right to me—like a song or the way the red leaves of the maple tree are shining—it's because that song or those leaves vibrate with a frequency that matches my frequency?"

Tripp smiles and shrugs. "Why not?"

She nods. "I like it. Maybe it explains something."

"What?"

"Maybe it explains the reason why one person likes another. It's because their souls both thrum at the same frequency."

They are leaning in toward each other, knees almost touching, the smile between them as intense as a flame. "To resonance," he says, and they tap their pencils as if they are glasses of champagne.

NOVEMBER 6. THURSDAY.

Broody's Rug & Carpet; 5:31 p.m.

Tripp/I'm at my mom's store. Remember the blasty rug?

Lyla/Yeah. Poor Henry!

Tripp/I checked the orders on the computer and found his address. I'm thinking about making a special delivery tomorrow night. . . . Want to join me in some criminal activity?

Lyla/Yes! Yes! Yes!

NOVEMBER 7. FRIDAY.

The Alley; 7:31 p.m.

The alley is narrow and dark with a rivulet of black, oily liquid running down the center and lined on either side with Dumpsters and empty cardboard boxes.

Tripp is waiting by the back door to Broody's Rug & Carpet, under the light. Lyla appears at the far end of the alley, sees him, and runs toward him. The collar of her short coat is turned up. She's wearing black mittens, a black beret, and, even though it's dark, big black sunglasses.

She starts laughing as soon as she is close enough to see him clearly.

"I like your disguise, Bonnie," Tripp calls out. "Why are you laughing? I'm supposed to look criminally

209

exciting." He adjusts his black knit cap and fake mustache.

"You look criminally insane. I like it."

"Here's the goods." He pats a rug, which is rolled and wrapped in plastic.

"Oooh. I want to see it!"

He rotates it so she can see the pomegranate-colored label.

"How did you get it out?" she asks.

"When my mom was busy, I set it out here. Then I told her I had to go and walked out the front door."

"Is she still in there? What if she comes out?"

"She never comes out back here. She's afraid of rats."

Lyla starts looking around nervously, and he laughs.

He pulls a piece of paper out of his back pocket. "Our destination is 830 Bradford Road. I mapquested it, and it's four miles away. That's a long walk."

"We shall take a cab!" Lyla announces.

"You keep suggesting that. Have you ever done it?"

"Not by myself. But my dad and I have done it in New York."

Lyla takes off her mittens and picks up one end of the rug, and Tripp grabs the other.

"I can't believe I'm doing this," Tripp whispers.

"It's like a dead body!" She starts laughing.

"Shh!"

By the time they walk the rug to the main street, they're

breathing hard. "This way, so my mom doesn't see us through the window." He pulls her to the left.

"It's so cold, I can see your breath," she says. She brings two fingers to her lips as if she's smoking a cigarette. "Bonnie and Clyde always light up after a heist."

After a few minutes, they manage to flag down a taxi. As it pulls over, Lyla takes off her sunglasses and points to Tripp's mustache. "Quick! We have to look normal or he'll freak."

He pulls it off and winces, and she laughs again.

The driver, a man with a bright orange turban, leans over as the passenger-side window rolls down. He looks at them suspiciously and says, "Show me, please, you have moneys."

They pull out enough money between the two of them and get in, the rug on their laps. It's slightly too long, so they roll down the window and stick one end out.

"One extra dollar for window," the driver says, accent thick.

"For opening the window?" Tripp asks.

Lyla elbows him. "Fine."

"We are going where?" the driver asks.

"830 Bradford Road," Tripp says.

As the cab pulls out, Lyla whispers, "It's a magic carpet ride."

The cabdriver looks in the rearview mirror and asks if they went rug shopping, except with his accent, it sounds like he says rug chopping.

Lyla and Tripp smile at each other. "We are redecorating," Lyla says.

"Indeed," Tripp adds.

Lyla's phone buzzes, signaling a text message. "Daddy checking in . . . he's asking if I'm warm enough," she says. "I'm cozy. Bake sale going well," she says as she texts. "Selling lots!" She leans toward Tripp and whispers, "Should we feel guilty for . . ."—she looks at the rug on their laps—"rug chopping?"

"This rug has been in our store for five years and nobody has bought it." He whispers. "So we are really doing the rug a favor."

Lyla laughs. "It will be loved by Henry."

"Henry is a little man with a mind of his own. Just my style."

"Henry's little mind is about to be blown."

Silently, they watch the passing lights out the window. After a while, Lyla starts to hum.

The driver smiles, warming to them, and says loudly, "Singing is a much pleasing thing."

"Indeed," Tripp and Lyla both say at the same time and try to keep from laughing.

"My cousin is a rock star in India," the driver says.

"Does he play the guitar?" Tripp asks.

"Sitar," the man says. "Strings, but not a guitar."

"We have a band," Lyla says. "It's called the Thrum Society."

"No kidding me?" the driver exclaims. "You are famous?"

"Not yet. But we have a gig."

"Sing me a song!" He stops at a light and looks back at them.

Lyla starts singing their waltz song, and Tripp joins in. The light turns green. The driver's head nods to their song.

"That was good!" he exclaims when they're done. "That was really good!" He hands Lyla a card. "My name is Aamod. Call me if you need a ride to your music gigs. No extra dollar for the window."

"How much would it cost for you to take us to Loblolly, Maryland, and back?"

"Never heard of this place."

"There's a theater there called the Pomegranate Playhouse," Lyla explains.

"Call me with the address and I can price you the quote."

Tripp and Lyla look at each other and smile.

The driver turns down a side street and slows down. "Which one is it?"

Tripp peers out. "Um . . . it's number 830. . . ."

"That one," Lyla says. "The one with the porch."

They pool their money and pay, then Lyla slides out with the rug, and Tripp follows. "Wave and look natural, like this is our house," Lyla whispers as the cab pulls away.

"I don't think people wave good-bye to their cab-drivers," Tripp says.

"He's not just our cabdriver. He's our fan." She waves.

The cab turns the corner, and the street is quiet. The air is freezing, and they both shiver. "What now, Bonnie?"

"We put it on the porch and run."

"We need to write his name on it."

"No, that'll seem like we're stalking."

"All right. How about 'From Santa'?"

Lyla laughs. "From the Thrum Society."

The porch light in the neighboring house goes on and Tripp panics, lunging toward the shadowy part of the lawn, pulling the rug and Lyla with him. His foot hits a skateboard and he goes down while the skateboard flies out from under him and bangs against the bottom step of the porch.

"Are you okay?" Lyla whispers, laughing.

"Ssh! Duck!"

Lyla crouches down as a man from the house next door walks to the street and gets in his car.

"If he looks up, he'll see us," Lyla whispers.

"Make like a lawn troll and freeze." Tripp's face takes on a ridiculous frozen grin.

Lyla laughs.

"Shh! Trolls don't laugh," he says through his teeth.

After the car disappears, they pick up the rug. When Tripp hits the first stair, it creaks noisily.

"Shh!" Lyla says.

"I can't help it," Tripp says. He sets his end of the rug on the porch and they slide it the rest of the way.

"Knock!"

"No. You knock!"

"Shh!"

"Same time."

They both tiptoe up, look at each other, start laughing, knock, and run.

Tripp looks back twice. The second time, he sees the front door open and someone step out. They run past houses, parked cars, and piles of fallen leaves. He pulls Lyla down a side street. A dog barks and they run faster, laughing.

"Do you know where we are?" Lyla asks, breathless.

"I think we need to turn left on the next street."

A police car enters the next intersection and turns toward them.

Lyla grabs Tripp's arm.

"Don't run," Tripp says. "Look completely natural. It's going to pass right by us."

Lyla's hand stays on his arm. "We're doomed, Clyde," she whispers. "We have guilt written all over us. We probably have rug fibers on our clothes!"

As they walk fast, past the headlights, Tripp starts to hum Lyla's guilt song.

"What are you doing?" Lyla whispers.

"I'm acting natural. People always hum a cheery tune when they walk down the street."

As soon as the patrol car is gone, Lyla bends over. "I wasn't breathing!"

"Come on." Tripp runs across the street and pulls Lyla with him.

When they hit the sidewalk on the other side, Lyla stops. "Look!" She stares straight up.

In the glow of the streetlight, specks dance in the sky.

Lyla brings her hand down. There is a snowflake on her outstretched fingertip. She holds it out to Tripp. "Confetti!"

"Yeah." He smiles. "The sky is throwing us a party."

NOVEMBER 12. WEDNESDAY.

Name: *Tripp Broody*

A—
Nice job,
Tripp

Unit Quiz: The Physics of Sound

1. A sound wave traveling through air is an example of a:

    a.   transverse wave.   c.   standing wave.

    (b.)   longitudinal wave.   d.   surface wave.

2. In which medium does sound travel the fastest?

    a.   salt water   c.   air

    b.   fresh water   (d.)   cast iron

3. A piano, violin, or guitar uses the resonance of a wooden soundboard to

    (a.)   amplify the sound.   c.   raise the pitch.

    b.   dampen the sound.   d.   limit standing waves.

4. An ambulance siren sounds different as it approaches you than when it moves away from you. What scientific term would you use to explain how this happens?

    a.   ultrasound   c.   rarefaction

    b.   diffraction   (d.)   the Doppler effect

NOVEMBER 21. FRIDAY.

Tripp/I think you should add cello to your Little Room song.

Lyla/I heard a violinist at the metro. I'm applying for a permit for us!

Hey Mr. Odd,
Annie joined the Canticle Quartet which makes it a Quintet. Even though we're still avoiding each other, I think it's great.
—Ms. Even

NEW SONG
ABOUT OUR RUG ADVENTURE

I got my ride

making a
clean getaway

today
obey
right of way

slip through
the alley

runaway
ride away
hideaway
my way
play croquet
DNA

get away

far
car

got to get away

STEALING

GET AWAY

stealing for good
like robin hood!

BONNIE AND CLYDE

pedal to
the metal

nice heist

steal rug, magic carpet

can't be late
celebrate fate

Get Away

Tripp, how's this for a start?

I'll be Bonnie, you be Clyde
Steal the snow out of the sky
Steal a joke and let it fly
Let it fly

Steal the show with your disguise
Hide away from prying eyes
Steal the fun and say surprise
Say surprise

I've got to get away somehow
I've got to get away right now

NOVEMBER 22. SATURDAY.

THE POMEGRANATE PLAYHOUSE; 11:31 A.M.

In the clearing on the right are an ancient-looking stone house and a beautiful wooden barn. Above the front doors of the barn is a big, brightly colored hand-painted sign: *THE POMEGRANATE PLAYHOUSE.*

After the cab pulls away, Tripp sets down the guitar case and turns to Lyla. "I can't do this," he says.

She picks up the case. "Yes, you can."

"You've played in front of billions of people. I haven't."

She pulls his arm. "Come on. We're going."

Cars are already parked on the grass next to the barn, and another car is just arriving. They head down a stone path decorated with pumpkins that have been scooped out and filled with wildflowers, catching a glimpse of water and a small dock with a rowboat through the woods. Inside the barn is a stage with an ornately painted proscenium and shimmering curtains that are pulled aside. A dozen people are already sitting in the audience. More are coming in behind them.

Lyla motions for Tripp to look on the walls. Large paintings of pomegranates line both sides of the room.

A man in a suit comes over, and Lyla explains who they are. "Mom," he calls to an old woman talking to another woman by the stage. "The musicians are here!"

The old woman walks over, wildflowers in her hands. Although her face is lined with wrinkles, her eyes are blue and disarmingly clear, and a thick white braid hangs over her shoulder. Her dress is wine-colored with bright splashes of white and blue. "I'm Ruby. You're the Thrum Society?" She is clearly surprised.

"If you don't want us to play—" Tripp pulls back, and Lyla elbows him.

"Of course I want you to play!" A smile lights her face. "I'm delighted! So young! What talent! Come in, come in! I know we said we'd start at noon, but as soon as everybody's here, we're going to dive right in."

"No rehearsal?" Lyla asks.

"You'll be great." She smiles, walking them up the side stairs onto the stage, where there are two chairs and microphones off to the right. A woman wearing a

222

ministerial robe walks onto the stage, adjusting her collar, and Ruby introduces them to her. "Romeo is going to play the accordion for the entrance and the exit. So just sit tight. After the vows, Reverend Liz will give you a nod and you can play your waltz. How does this setup look? Need anything else?"

Tripp and Lyla look at each other. "Looks fine," Lyla says.

More people come in, and Ruby squeals with delight and rushes off to greet them.

Tripp and Lyla sit down.

"I didn't think we'd be on a stage," Tripp whispers. "I feel like everybody is looking at us."

Finally, just after all the seats fill, Reverend Liz stands in the center of the stage and looks at the doorway with an expectant smile. A tiny old man appears in the frame with a small button accordion, wearing a striped tuxedo with tails and a top hat. At first, it appears as though he is too frail to move, but he begins to play the accordion and does a funny shuffling dance up the aisle, stopping halfway to catch his breath. When he gets to the stairs leading up to the stage, he stops and gives a shrug and smile, saying in an Italian accent, "A long way up, no?"

Everybody laughs. Ruby's son and another man get one of the chairs from the stage and bring it down to him. After he sits, they carry the chair, with him in it, up the stairs and set it onstage.

Romeo plays louder and everyone turns to face the doorway.

Ruby appears with the wildflowers in her hands. She smiles at everyone as she walks down the aisle and up the stage steps to take the chair next to Romeo.

"Can I kiss my bride now?" the old man asks Reverend Liz. "Because maybe I don't make it to the end."

Everybody cheers them on, and he and Ruby share a kiss.

"I didn't think she was the bride," Lyla whispers.

"Me neither," Tripp whispers back.

While the minister tells the story of how Ruby and Romeo met in Italy when Ruby wandered into a gallery and saw his paintings of pomegranates, Tripp thinks about how perfect and happy they look together. Then it's time for the vows, and he can feel the nervousness approaching like a tidal wave; at any moment, the minister will be turning to give them the cue to sing. But the way Romeo takes Ruby's face in his hands and looks straight into her eyes catches Tripp off guard. He was expecting the standard recitation of vows; instead, Romeo is speaking in a voice that—even though Tripp can't understand the words—seems to be springing directly from the old man's heart. *"Prometto di ascoltarti quando sei triste e di ridere con te quando sei felice."* Romeo puts his hand on his chest. "I feel you in here, Ruby. And no matter what happens, I will always love you." He smiles and puts a ring on her finger.

Ruby wipes away a tear and kisses him and whispers, "How did I get so lucky?"

He shrugs and she laughs. Then, through her tears, she says, "I, Ruby, take you, Romeo, to be my husband. I promise to listen to you when you are sad and to laugh with you when you are happy. I feel you in my heart. And no matter what happens, I will always love you." She puts a ring on his finger.

They kiss.

The minister nods at Tripp and Lyla to play their song.

Tripp feels all the blood rush from his head as the room grows silent and all eyes turn to them. He cannot possibly sing, and then he looks at Lyla, and her smile is like a hand on his arm. He takes a breath and starts to play. They sing the first few notes, and the familiar sound of their voices together gives him an added breath of confidence. His body relaxes and he lets the song pour out, their voices surging in harmony. It is the first time they have ever played in a large, open room; and, as their sound fills the room, it seems to join forces with the love that is emanating from Ruby and Romeo and the love that is pouring out of the entire audience, and it fills a space inside Tripp's chest and makes him feel more alive than he has ever felt.

When the last note ends, the silence that comes after it feels holy. He looks at Lyla. Her eyes are glistening, and she gives him a secret smile. They did it.

"I now pronounce you husband and wife!" the minister exclaims.

After Romeo and Ruby kiss, Romeo picks up his accordion and starts to play. Ruby's son and other men jump onstage and lift up both Ruby and Romeo in their chairs and carry them around while everyone follows, dancing and clapping, in a line.

Lyla jumps up and grabs Tripp's hand and they join the line. Lyla looks as if she couldn't possibly be happier, and it makes Tripp laugh out loud.

"What's so funny?" she yells over the noise.

He grins and shakes his head, unable to explain it.

The whole procession spills out of the barn, and when the song is over, Ruby invites everyone inside to eat lunch in the house, to return to the barn for more dancing, or to take the rowboat out for a ride.

"Let's take the boat out before it's time for the cab to come," Tripp suggests.

Lyla grabs the guitar and they head down to the dock.

Bordered on all sides by pine trees, the lake is full of small inlets edged with marsh grasses. Tripp rows, and Lyla sits opposite him with the guitar in her lap. They glide, listening to the splash of the oars and the creak of the boat, and then she starts to play. When they get to the middle of the lake, the gathering clouds drift over half of the sun, creating a ray that illuminates a path on the water. She stops and gives the guitar to Tripp. He starts to play the chords she was playing, but plucks a rhythm that he has never tried before.

She leans forward. "I like how that sounds. Play it again."

He repeats the rhythm.

"We need to make up a new song," she says.

"What should it be about?"

She looks across the water and says, "All this."

"The lake?"

She smiles. "This feeling. This whole day has been so cool. I feel so lucky." The boat rocks gently.

He stops playing. "Did you ever think about how if I had been assigned to Room A instead of Room B, you wouldn't have seen my trash or the guitar, and we wouldn't have started writing notes, and we wouldn't be here right now?"

She nods. "That's what I mean. I feel lucky."

"*Trash is so lucky*," he sings and strums.

She laughs. "I want it to be a thrumming song. . . . When we were singing in there . . ."

He looks up.

". . . I felt like all our souls were thrumming at the same frequency." Her eyes are bright. "Yours. Mine. Ruby's. Romeo's. Everybody's."

He knew she felt the same way he did. He plays the chord progression again and sings, "*Lucky, lucky me*."

"I like it!" she says. "That should be in the chorus. Let's get it down before we forget." She reaches into her coat pocket and produces her digital recorder with a smile. "I'm like a Girl Scout. Always prepared." They sing it again and she records it.

"Let's have a verse that is kind of sad and then when it gets to the chorus, it's happy."

"I can do sad." He strums and sings, *"Before today, my days were blue. I was locked in a closet . . ."*

". . . with mops and shampoo . . ." Lyla laughs.

". . . and a kangaroo," he adds, *"and a stinkin' shoe . . ."*

They start to experiment with different lines when they hear a voice.

"Lyla!"

It sends a shock through them at the same time. They look back toward the dock, and there, against the backdrop of the darkening sky, is Lyla's dad.

"Oh, this is not good," Lyla says.

"How did he find us?"

"Lyla!" her dad calls again.

"What should we do?" Tripp asks.

"What do you mean? What choice do we have? We have to row back." Lyla takes the guitar from him.

Tripp grabs the oars and begins turning the boat around as Lyla pulls out her phone and turns it on. Fifteen messages. "He must have found out I wasn't at school," Lyla says.

"What did you tell him?"

"That I was at a French club thing. I should've known this wouldn't work."

"But how did he find out we're here?"

"He must have read all our messages on my computer."

"He has your password?"

She nods. "He made it a rule that he has to have it, but I never thought he'd actually go snooping."

They fall silent as they approach the dock. Her father yells as soon as they get close enough to hear. "This is the most irresponsible thing—"

Tripp winces and keeps rowing.

"We were just coming in. I swear," Lyla says, her voice thick and anxious. "We were planning on being back in time—"

"I called fifteen times."

She holds up her phone. "I was just about to call you, Dad. Please don't overreact. . . ."

Tripp has rowed too hard; he plunges one oar in the water to turn the boat, but the bow slams against a dock post.

Mr. Marks crouches down. Holding the post with one arm, he reaches out and grabs the rope on the bow. "I know about everything," he says. "The lies . . . the secret meetings . . . stealing the guitar from school and the money from me that was supposed to go toward lessons. . . ." He throws a disgusted look at Tripp. "All this ugliness is stopping right now."

Tripp flinches. "It's not—"

"You don't have the right to say a single word," Mr. Marks says. "This friendship is over. I've already taken steps. . . ." With one hand he pulls the rope so that the rowboat glides against the dock, then he reaches down and steadies it with the other hand. "Come on, Lyla. We're leaving right now." He glances back at Tripp. "Your mom knows, too, by the way."

Lyla hands Tripp the guitar. The rock of the boat as she steps out breaks his heart. *Tell him, Lyla. Please tell him that it wasn't ugly.*

Mr. Marks puts his arm around Lyla and leads her away. Lyla turns back and looks at Tripp, her eyes full of tears. Tripp sits in the boat and watches as they walk up the path and out of sight, everything good inside him draining out.

He pulls out his phone, turns it on, types in a message to her, and hits SEND, but it bounces back. *Message failed.* He tries again and again. Could Mr. Marks have blocked his number from Lyla's phone? Is that what he meant by "already taken steps"?

Lyla's digital recorder is on the seat. As he picks it up and puts it in his pocket, his phone buzzes. Mom calling. Reluctantly, he answers. "Yeah?"

Her exhale is loud. "Finally. Somebody named Lyla's dad called me up and basically told me what a horrible person you are."

"It's not what you think—"

"I don't know what's going on. It was humiliating, Tripp. I'm on my way—I'm at a red light. When I get there, we're going to—"

"You don't have to come. There's a cab coming—"

"A cab?"

"It's how we came. We already paid him for the return trip. He's coming back at—"

"You're not taking a cab. I'll be there in half an hour."

"Mom—"

"The light turned green. I have to go. I'm hanging up."

Tripp slides his phone closed. He sits for a long minute, staring at the water. Then he reluctantly gets out. On his way past the house, Ruby's son stops him and hands him an envelope with cash and tells him how much they enjoyed their music. Guitar in hand, he heads up the driveway to the road and sits on a tree stump. He calls Aamod, who is already on his way, and cancels.

"No refund," Aamod says.

"Yeah, I know." Tripp replies.

A raindrop lands on his hand, and he looks up at the clouds.

The Markses' Car; 3:14 p.m.

Mr. Marks's voice is stretched thin. "We can make it. I have your cello and dress clothes in the backseat. We'll go straight there and you can change and have a good forty minutes to warm up." He leans forward and wipes the condensation collecting on the inside of the windshield.

Lyla looks at the raindrops on the window. The beauty

of the wedding ceremony, of their music, and of the boat ride with Tripp seem like scenes from a play. She didn't stick up for Tripp. She left without even saying good-bye. Tripp must think she is a coward.

"Lyla?" Her father's voice cracks. His hands are gripping the wheel, his eyes are brimming with tears. "Lyla, I don't understand how you could do something like this today. Didn't you realize how worried I'd be?"

One raindrop pools into another and they form a narrow river running down her window.

"It's like you don't even care about the audition," her father continues. "This is so unlike you."

"I told you," Lyla says. "We arranged for a cab to get us. I would've gotten home on time."

"On time!? On the day of a big audition, you do not go running away from home and playing around with—"

"I wasn't running away from home. I was—"

"This whole guitar thing. I know you feel sorry for this boy, for whatever he's been through, but he is trouble. . . ."

Lyla closes her eyes.

"That's the thing about your age group," he goes on. "One day you like this . . . the next day you like that . . . but you can't let an opportunity like Coles slip by and regret it."

She can't breathe.

The road curves sharply and he brakes and swerves to follow it.

She pulls out her phone and checks her messages.

They are all from her dad. Nothing from Tripp yet. She starts typing a new message.

"You're not texting him," he says.

"Dad—"

"I blocked his number from your phone."

"Dad, you can't just do that—"

"Lyla." Her dad flicks on the windshield wipers and leans forward. "Hold on. See that piece of paper? I wrote down the directions. What's the name of the next road? Pine Top?"

"Dad, you can't just block people from my phone."

"Lyla, a friendship with that boy is not a good idea." The road curves again, and he passes a turnoff for another road. "I think that was Pine Top. Look at the directions, please, and tell me if I should find a place to turn around."

"Dad, you don't understand. Tripp isn't a bad person—"

"Lyla, I don't think you're in a position to judge—"

The road curves again and, between one sweep of the wiper's arm, Lyla sees the deer leap from the woods onto the asphalt: the pronged antlers, the muscular haunches, the delicate legs.

She knows the instant she sees the deer that it is too late. Her father slams on the brakes, and the car begins to spin out of control. Lyla hears a scream, and she doesn't know if it's coming from her father, herself, the deer, or the screeching tires.

But I'm not ready to die, she thinks; and in that split

second, she imagines she is still sitting in the rowboat, playing the guitar with Tripp, the boat rocking gently on the surface of the water.

The deer touches down just inches beyond the car and leaps again, his back hoof clearing the bumper. The car swerves off the road and heads for a large pine tree. Lyla braces herself as the tree seems to rush forward to meet them. A crack as loud as the splitting of the earth hits her ears as they crash. The spinning stops, and then the world goes silent.

The deer is gone.

THE BROODYS' CAR; 3:21 P.M.

"Enlighten me, Tripp," his mom says as she drives. "How on earth did you talk this poor girl into stealing a guitar from school and skimming money from her dad's pocket so that you could take a sixty-minute cab ride to—"

"It wasn't like that. You're making it sound like I'm—"

"I'm just relaying what her dad said to me. Do you have any idea what it's like to have a complete stranger call you up and tell you, essentially, that your kid is a criminal and that you are a bad parent?"

"I'm *not* a criminal."

"According to Mr. Marks, this girl was a perfect student until you came along. He called you a 'terrible influence.'" His mother's voice rages on like a fire. "He

234

wants you to stay as far away from his daughter as is humanly possible. What is wrong with you?"

"We're friends. We—"

"Oh, come on."

"What? You don't believe I have a friend?"

"Frankly, I don't. You haven't made an effort since Josh moved away. That was a year and a half ago, Tripp."

"Well, she's a friend. I have a friend."

"More like you have someone who can get you a precious guitar."

Tripp looks out the window.

The sky opens, and the rain pours.

"No, really. I'm waiting to be enlightened, Tripp. Explain what this supposed music gig was all about. You expect me to believe that someone would hire a kid they don't even know to play at something as important as a wedding?"

"I'm not just a kid. And they're really nice people—"

"—who could have been ax murderers. Did you ever think of that?" She throws him a look. "Did you ever think that somebody could have been posing as a bride and groom to get you to lure this girl out and kidnap her? Reckless and dangerous." She shakes her head.

Through the rain, he watches the blur of passing trees. He will not bother to explain anything to her. She just shoots him down as soon as he starts to talk.

"You're going to write a letter of apology to that girl's

father and pay him back the money that you basically stole from him for this cab ride. I'll drive you to their house tomorrow night and you can deliver it personally. On Monday, you're going to return the guitar to school with an apology to that music teacher. You're going to report to the store every day after school to do your homework. No ifs, ands, or buts. And Thanksgiving weekend, I expect you to work for me." She throws another hard glance. "You're going to Crenshaw if they accept you." The road curves. She turns right onto Pine Top Road and heads toward home.

THE MARKSES' CAR; 3:24 P.M.

"Lyla?" Her father's voice is frantic. "Lyla?"

When Lyla opens her eyes, she sees a jumble of images like pieces of a jigsaw puzzle that have been dumped into one pile. Jagged metal on her left leg and a tree branch where the window should be. Diamonds are scattered everywhere and a red river is running over her and dripping into her lap.

She tries to move her head, and the pain rips through her. Her eyes close and she feels herself sinking even though she is pinned against the seat. The rain is pouring down her neck, and she decides that she must be in the lake. *It's so cold*, she says, but her lips don't move.

Pinned to the seat next to her, her father manages to

pull his cell phone out of his pocket to dial 911. "Yes, it's an emergency. An accident. We need an ambulance. My daughter . . ." He is breathless.

She hears his voice. *He must be swimming, she thinks, trying to hold his head above the water. Is he talking about me? Am I the daughter? I should call out to him. . . .*

She feels as if she is sinking into dark green water.

TRIPP'S ROOM; 5:13 P.M.

<To: Lyla Marks> November 22

Lyla, I think your dad blocked my number from your phone. Please, please meet me in the tree house tomorrow. Tomorrow night my mom is driving me to your house to deliver an apology and the money we took from your lessons. On Monday, I have to return the school guitar. That reminds me. I have the money from the gig. They paid us in cash. I have it in my wallet and I want you to have it. I'll give it to you at school on Monday. Please write back. I'm going crazy.—Tripp

NOVEMBER 23. SUNDAY.

TRIPP'S ROOM; 1:37 P.M.

Dear Mr. Marks,
~~Please accept this apology. I'm sorry for being alive.~~

Dear Mr. Marks,
~~Please accept this apology. And please stop forcing the cello down your daughter's throat. This will damage her singing voice, which is really beautiful.~~

Dear Mr. Marks,

I'm sorry for ~~encouraging your daughter to let her soul thrum.~~

Dear Mr. Marks,

Why ~~don't you play~~ the cello and leave Lyla ~~alone?~~

Dear Mr. Marks,

Please ~~don't take~~ Lyla away. She is my ~~best~~ friend.

Dear Mr. Marks,

I am sorry about all the secrets. Please don't be mad at Lyla. I'm not a criminal and I wasn't using her. We became friends, and we started playing the guitar together and writing songs together, and it was a good thing. Lyla is an amazing songwriter, and she was also helping me with my homework, which was genuinely nice because I started to really like science. But I know you're upset because all these things were keeping her from playing the cello.

Please accept this apology.

−Tripp Broody

Tripp's Room; 8:57 p.m.

<To: Lyla Marks> November 23

Lyla, I waited all day. Are you mad at me? I get the fact that your dad probably blocked my phone number and my e-mail address, but I thought you'd find some way to talk to me. My mom drove me to your house, but no one was home. She didn't want me to leave cash, but I left a note for your dad. I hope it helps. Tell him my mom is going to mail a check. I'm having a panic attack that he has taken you away and locked you up someplace. Did you do the audition yesterday? Please find a way to tell me what's going on. Tomorrow I'm going to the grocery store to stock up on pomegranates. If your dad won't let me see you, I'm going to lob them at his head. We have to finish our thrumming song. I have your digital recorder.—Tripp

Hospital; 8:58 p.m.

Down a gleaming white corridor through a set of double doors marked SURGICAL INTENSIVE CARE UNIT, Lyla is lying in a bed, slightly upright, with her arms at her

240

sides, bound to the metal rails to keep her from moving. Her face is swollen, and her eyelids are purple and puffy. Her head is shaved, and underneath the bandage, a piece of her skull has been removed. A breathing tube is in her mouth, held in place by white tape. A trickle of liquid is snaking out her right ear and down her neck. A thinner tube is taped to her right arm and connected to a bag that is hanging from a silver stand. Through the needle in her arm, cold liquid drips into her veins, medicine to reduce the swelling of her brain and to keep her asleep, and fluids to keep her hydrated. Underneath the blue hospital blanket, her left leg is in a cast. The hiss of the ventilator fills the room.

She is somewhere past a dream, floating in a dark green lake. Hour after hour, the current gently tries to pull her farther away.

NOVEMBER 24. MONDAY.

ORCHESTRA ROOM; 8:13 A.M.

Tripp walks into the music room with the guitar and a note of apology. It's an even day, which means Lyla should be coming to the orchestra room first period, so he is hoping she will walk through the door and smile.

Instead, he overhears Mr. Jacoby talking with Mr. Sanders about the accident. Bit by bit he pieces together what has happened to Lyla, then Mr. Jacoby notices him and stops talking. The teacher takes the guitar and the note and pauses, as if he doesn't know what to say. Finally, he gives him a nod and tells him to go to class.

Tripp walks out in a daze. Ahead, he sees Annie approaching and he stops her.

She looks sick to her stomach and says, "I don't want to talk about it."

The bell rings and she hurries into the music room.

"I'm sure you have somewhere to go, Tripp," Mr. Handlon says as he walks by.

Tripp walks to class and sits down. He wants to scream, but he is locked in the reality of this classroom, this day.

He gets through his morning classes. At lunch, he calls Lyla even though he knows it's pointless, and then he writes three notes to Annie, asking her to tell him what she knows, but he throws them all away. By the afternoon, differing rumors about Lyla's accident are all over school. She has a broken leg. She has a concussion. She is going to be all right. She is dying.

As soon as school is over, his mom calls and reminds him that he has to come to the store. When he gets there, she peppers him with meaningless questions. Did you give the guitar back with an apology? Yes. Do you have your algebra book? Yes. Do you know what you're supposed to do for science? Yes.

He goes into the back workroom and enters his zip code and the word *hospital* in a search engine on the computer. Fifteen hospitals are listed. He calls each one and asks if there is a patient named Lyla Marks. No each time. A thought occurs to him. He puts in the address for the Pomegranate Playhouse and finds the nearest hospital. He calls it, and the woman on the end of the line tells him that she's there. Time seems to stop.

"Is she okay?"

"Are you a family member?"

"I'm a friend."

"Information about this patient is unavailable at this time."

"Why? Can't you just tell me if she's going to be okay?"

"I'm sorry," the woman says. "It says here that family members only should have access to patient information."

He doesn't know what to do. To keep his mom off his back, he does his homework.

As soon as they get home, he disappears into his room. He listens to the recording that they made on the boat, their voices singing *lucky, lucky me*, and then he switches it off. It's like a horrible taunt.

NOVEMBER 25. TUESDAY.

Rockland School; 8:11 a.m.

A group of girls from Advanced Orchestra put a big white basket and a note about Lyla by the music room. Three stuffed animals are in the basket as well as cards that people are signing. Someone is going to bring it to the hospital tomorrow.

All day he hears more rumors. Lyla is in a coma. Lyla is brain-dead.

Annie is absent, and someone says she's visiting Lyla. Someone else says Annie's at home, sick because she's worried that Lyla is going to die hating her. She and Lyla were in a big fight over him. People are talking. No one talks to him directly, but they know that he and Lyla were caught in the music room together; they know that they were eating lunch together. People are looking at him strangely. Like maybe he is to blame. Then he hears Marisse say that the reason Annie is sick is because she thinks she caused the accident: that day she had called Marisse and confessed that she was hoping that Lyla wouldn't make it to the Coles audition. It was like a jinx, Marisse says.

As soon as school is out, Tripp leaves. He calls Lyla's home phone number and listens to the recorded message. "You've reached the Marks residence. Please leave your name and number after the beep."

Tripp takes a breath. "This is Tripp Broody. . . . I know I'm not supposed to call. But I just need to know how Lyla is. This is my cell phone number. Please call back."

NOVEMBER 26. WEDNESDAY.

Rockland School; 8:21 a.m.

Tripp hears from Mr. Sanders that Lyla was transferred to a special hospital nearby. He says that Lyla isn't snapping out of it; yes — it's really a coma. Tripp wants to ask what that means, but he is too afraid.

At lunchtime, he sees Annie in the hallway and hears that she and another girl are going to take the basket, overflowing now with stuffed animals, to the hospital after school today. All day he wants to put a note in the basket, but he is worried that Mr. Marks will read it and get even more angry.

TRIPP'S ROOM; 7:53 P.M.

Tripp is sitting at his desk, reading articles about comas on the web. People in comas can often hear, but they can't get a certain part of the brain to wake up, so they can't respond. He clicks on a story about a woman who was in a car accident at the age of twenty-six and never woke up. The story hits him like a kick to the stomach.

The door to his room opens, and his mom walks in, oblivious to what he's going through. "I just got an e-mail from Crenshaw about your status." She holds up a print-out. "We have to talk about this sooner or later, so it might as well be sooner."

He holds his breath and stares at his screen, trying to keep from falling apart.

"So you're not talking? Is that it, Tripp?"

"Please just leave me alone, Mom."

"Don't give me that attitude."

Her voice shoves against him, and his composure breaks. He gets up, sending his chair to the floor with a crash, and meets his mother's gaze. "Lyla got in a car accident on the way home from the wedding. Okay, Mom? And I don't know if she's going to be all right."

He pushes past her, walks out the back door and down the steps, and stands in the backyard. The ground under his feet is cold, the air, too—he can see his breath. No moon. No stars. Nothing but black. Why is it that everything he loves gets taken away from him? It's like there's a black hole in the sky with his name on it and its job is to suck everything that he loves out of existence.

Lining either side of the concrete patio are rows of autumn mums in clay flowerpots, and the cheerful symmetry, for some reason, makes him even angrier. He picks up a flowerpot and hurls it at their fence. Even as the satisfying crash hits his ears, he knows that it is pointless. The flowerpots are not to blame. He picks up another and throws it anyway and then another, until all six are broken, and finally he sits on the bottom step.

After a few minutes, he hears the sound of the door opening behind him. His mom walks down the stairs and sits next to him, hugging herself to stay warm. She sees the broken pots and says nothing about them. Finally, she speaks. "I called Tina Chan, a mom I know from last year's silent auction committee to see if she had any information about Lyla. I remember that she was involved with the music program and thought she might know Lyla's family."

Tripp doesn't move.

"A deer jumped in front of the Markses' car, Tripp. I don't want you to blame yourself or Lyla's dad, for that matter. It's nobody's fault. It just happened."

Tripp takes this in. "Is she going to be okay?"

"Kids are resilient. I bet she'll get better soon."

He looks at the broken pots. "That means you don't know."

She is silent. "Yeah. I don't know, Tripp. It's definitely a serious injury."

He lets his breath out in a small stream. "I want to go to the hospital."

She puts an arm around his shoulder. "It's really nice that you want to visit her, Tripp. Really nice. But . . . I don't know . . . her dad must be so overwhelmed, and it might upset him. I don't think we should be adding tension to the situation, do you?"

Tripp looks at the black sky.

She pats his leg. "It's freezing. Come inside."

He nods, but he doesn't move.

"You know you can't go around breaking flowerpots, either." She attempts a smile. He nods again. "Come inside, honey."

"In a minute."

She goes in, and he closes his eyes.

Lyla . . . just wake up. Please.

HOSPITAL; 9:06 P.M.

"Sweetie, feel this. Feel how soft it is." Lyla's dad picks up her hand and slips a small stuffed teddy bear underneath it. "Feel that? If you can hear my voice, just wiggle your fingers."

The voice washes over her. She has sunk to the bottom of the lake, too deep for the voice to reach her.

"The doctor said the swelling is gone. The medicine is out of your system. All you have to do is open your eyes. . . ." His voice chokes. "Sweetie, please . . ."

NOVEMBER 27. THURSDAY.

THE BROODYS' CAR; 3:07 P.M.

The drive to Aunt Gertrude's is long and quiet. It's Thanksgiving. Tripp thinks about Lyla, and Ruby, and Romeo, and Annie, and even Benjamin Fink, but mostly he thinks about Lyla and how much he misses her. He imagines her in the hospital, and his body aches. Over and over, he says her name in his mind. His mom had said nobody was to blame for the accident and maybe that's true. But Lyla's life might have been better if she hadn't met him, and this is the thought that makes him the saddest. She would not have been on that road, and the deer would not have crossed her path, and she and Annie wouldn't have gotten into such a big fight, and she would have aced the Coles audition and would live happily ever after. He should've stayed away. That was the trick. To stay separate from people. Keep a block of ice around his soul. Don't dream. Don't sing. Don't thrum.

"You can turn on the radio if you want," his mother says from the driver's seat.

He shakes his head, leans against the window, and closes his eyes.

Lucky, lucky me. He hates the fact that they were singing that in the boat right before the accident. He isn't lucky at all. He is cursed, and he brought that to Lyla. Just when he feels he won't be able to breathe, his mom turns to him.

"Tripp," she says gently. "If you want, I can try calling Tina Chan later today to see if I can get an update."

He takes in a small silent breath of gratitude and nods his head, and she seems to know that he can't say or do anything more than this.

Aunt Gertrude's House; 7:33 p.m.

Just after dinner, Tripp's mom steps into Aunt Gertrude's foyer to make the call. Tripp follows her and waits until she is done.

"She is off the ventilator, which means she is breathing on her own. She's also swallowing, which is good," she

253

says. "And she's getting really great care. The best doctors are on it." She has chosen her words carefully and she tries to smile.

Tripp knows she's trying to make him feel better, but he can see through it. If Lyla were improving, she wouldn't need the best doctors.

NOVEMBER 30. SUNDAY.

Broody's Rug & Carpet; 2:37 p.m.

Tripp is in the back workroom. He is supposed to be tossing the old samples into the Dumpster in the alley, but he is pacing. Since Thursday, every report about Lyla has been the same: no change. She isn't waking up.

His mom has been more sympathetic, but she doesn't really know who Lyla is or what their friendship was like. She has made it clear that she thinks the way to handle the tension is to keep on track with work. Neither of them has mentioned Crenshaw or the guitar. He can't talk about anything. He can't escape from the feeling that he brought nothing but trouble to Lyla. *Lucky, lucky me.*

As he passes the closet where his guitar is hidden, he bangs the padlock angrily.

After a few laps, he goes to the computer and checks his e-mail. He isn't expecting anything, and so it is a shock to see something in his in-box after all.

To: TrippBroody
From: JamesDarling
Date: November 30
Re: Wedding video
Attach: PSsong.wmv

Hi. Thought you might enjoy this video clip of you singing. You guys blew us all away. You added so much to the experience. We're really grateful you could share your music with us all. Thanks again.
—Jimmy (Ruby's son)

Tripp clicks on the video and it begins to play. Framed in the small video window are Ruby and Romeo sitting side by side on the stage, beaming, in the crazy elegance of the barn; and then the camera shifts and focuses on Lyla and him with the guitar. He can see the nervousness that he was trying to hide, and then Lyla smiles at him, and he feels that rush of warmth again, as if she is smiling at him right now. They start to play and their voices rise together; and, as he watches, an intense ripple of joy dances across his heart. The song pulses through him and lifts him, and he can't move until it's over. He plays it again and again.

When he finally turns it off, the silence seems to draw the walls of the workroom closer toward one another. He flashes back to the night his dad died in the hospital, to that feeling of helplessness he felt when he was sitting at home. He can't just sit here and do nothing. He opens the back door, looking out at the alley as if he'll see Lyla there in her Bonnie beret, blowing fake smoke through her lips. Puddles gleam on the black asphalt. A cat pokes through the empty boxes next to the Dumpster.

Lost, he closes the door, pulls Lyla's digital recorder and earbuds out of his backpack, and listens again to them singing in the boat, while he paces between the carpet remnants, the tool bench, and the trash bins. *Lucky, lucky me.* This time, instead of hearing the words as a taunt, he hears the joy in their voices as an undeniable truth. They were lucky to find each other. Nobody could take that away.

Grabbing a piece of paper out of the recycling bin, he starts working on the new song. He starts to pace again, singing it to himself, jotting down the lyrics as they come, reading the song over and over and adding more. When he's done, he stuffs it into his back pocket and walks into the showroom. His mom is behind the sales counter, thumbing through a stack of bills.

"Mom." He takes a breath. "Please open the closet. I'm going to get my guitar and I'm going to the hospital."

Her shoulders sag. "Tripp."

"I'm asking nicely."

"Tripp, I'm sure your intentions—" The bell on the front door jingles, and two women walk in. Tripp's mom looks at him with pity, but he can tell she isn't going to give. "You can't barge in on a family at a time like this. We need to give it more time. We'll talk about it in a few minutes," she whispers, and turns to greet the customers.

She is wrong. She was wrong about not letting him see his dad in the hospital, and she is wrong about this. He walks into the back room and picks up a crowbar. He sticks one end between the closet door and its frame and pushes. The door doesn't budge, but a dent appears in the frame. He tries again. Then he holds it with one hand, steps back, and gives the crowbar a good hard kick. The wood of the door frame splinters, but the lock is still in place. He wedges the end of the crowbar right against the tongue of the lock and kicks it again. The door pops open.

His guitar is in the back, in its case, between a mop and a bucket. He grabs it and walks out just as his mom is heading in to see what the noise was about.

"I have to go," he says.

"Tripp!" his mom calls out, but he keeps walking out the door, his heart pounding. The guitar case feels so right in his hand. "Tripp! Wait!"

He runs for a full block without looking back and then stops and pulls out his wallet. Luckily, he never took the wedding money out. He catches the next cab he sees.

When he arrives at the hospital, he tells the woman at

the visitor's desk that he is Lyla Marks's brother—just in case they only allow family—and she gives him the room number. When he gets to the third floor, he sees Mr. Marks, back toward him, talking with several people at the nurses' station in the middle of the hallway. Room 302 is on the right. He ducks in without being seen, and there is Lyla, lying still, a row of small stuffed animals lining either side of her bed.

He can't look at her.

The basket from school is on a table next to her bed. Above it, a bouquet of blue foil balloons kiss the ceiling, their strings tied to the basket handle. Curtains are drawn against the window. A stack of get-well cards is sitting on the chair. He walks around her bed, sets down his guitar case, and gets out his guitar. When he finally turns and wills himself to look at her, his throat burns.

Lyla's face is so still, she doesn't seem real. Her arms are on top of the blanket. An IV tube is attached to her right hand, which is bruised, and the other arm is bandaged. She looks so different, so fragile, like if he touched her, she might crumble.

A part of him is so scared he wants to leave, but he fights the fear and keeps his eyes on her face. He remembers the articles he read describing how people in comas can often hear, even if they can't respond. It takes him a minute to work up the courage to say her name out loud, and when he does, it comes out in barely a whisper.

"Lyla . . . look . . ." He holds up the guitar, lifts the

strap over his head, and manages a shaky smile. "I broke the door down, Lyla."

No response.

One at a time, he plucks each string, tuning as he goes. He strums it once and lets the sound fill the quiet of the room.

A yellow bruise still runs the entire length of the left side of her face, but the curve of her ear facing him is untouched and perfect.

He clears his throat and tries to get rid of the shakiness in his voice, to speak louder. "Lyla, it's me, Tripp. We were in the middle of making up a new song, remember?" He thinks about how bright her eyes looked that day on the lake. "I worked on it, Lyla. So you have to wake up and listen." He stops and pulls her digital recorder out of his pocket. "I'm going to record this. I came prepared . . . like a Girl Scout." He manages a quick laugh and turns it on, gently setting it next to her arm on the bed. "I'm going to leave the recorder here so you can listen to it anytime you want, okay? All our songs are on here, too. Okay?"

Her face is still. Her eyelashes are curved and pretty, the light on the wall behind her bed throwing tiny shadows of them on her skin.

Open your eyes, Lyla. Just open your eyes. His throat closes and his eyes fill with tears. He blinks them back and leans in closer. "I really need you to wake up, Lyla. I'm hearing a harmony on this. It doesn't sound good with just me. It needs your voice."

The room is silent.

"You said . . . in the boat . . . you said that you wanted the verse to be sad and then the chorus to be happy, so that's what I tried to do." When he starts to play, his fingers falter and he stops. He closes his eyes. Then he takes a breath and starts again.

As he sings, he imagines that he is pouring all of his energy into the air. He imagines that it is entering her ear and filling her, waking her up, molecule by molecule. He sings with everything he's got, and when he's done, he opens his eyes and sees his mom standing inside the doorway, tears streaming down her face. She can hardly get the words out, but Tripp understands her.

She says, "That was beautiful."

Tripp looks at Lyla and starts to cry. Then he looks back up at his mom. "She has to wake up," he says.

She nods through her tears.

The door opens, and Lyla's dad walks in, speechless.

"I'm sorry." Tripp wipes his face quickly. He fumbles to put his guitar back in the case and then he stops and slips his pick under Lyla's hand. He looks at her one more time. Then he grabs his case and walks out, his head buzzing, his feet unable to feel the floor.

Just as the elevator door is opening, his mother arrives behind him. She doesn't say a word, but she puts her arm around his shoulders and she holds him against her side.

After the small thump signals their arrival at the lobby and while they're waiting for the elevator doors to open, the words spill out. "None of it was ugly, Mom."

Her words come back quickly. "I can see that."

The doors open and she reaches into her pocket and takes out a tissue, which she hands to him, and then she picks up his guitar case. "Don't worry. I'm just carrying it to the car, not stealing it." She laughs as she wipes away her own tears and steps out.

Still in the elevator, he laughs and then he thinks of Lyla and starts to cry again, and his mom dives back in, stopping the doors with the guitar, to hug him.

HOSPITAL; 6:36 P.M.

"Lyla?" Her dad's voice is a whisper.

He pulls the chair close to her bed, and when he tries to hold her hand, he finds the red guitar pick that Tripp has left. One word is written on it in permanent marker: *Thrum.*

He puts the pick back in her hand and folds her fingers over it. Then he gently puts an earbud in each of her ears and pushes the play button on the recorder.

The sound of the guitar comes first and then Tripp's voice.

> *The sun was tied up in clouds*
> *And the moon wrung out of its songs.*
> *Up on Twelfth Street the trees were just trees*

262

Holding nothing but leaves in their arms.
All my days were locked in a closet with the
Rags and the brooms and the mops,
Nothing to feel but the feel of nothing
Slipping through keyholes and locks.

But you know what I need,
You strum against my strings
And make me sing,
Sing lucky, lucky me,
Sing lucky, lucky me.

The music rides on a wave into her.

You were telling your little white lie,
Making everybody happy, crying inside,
Staying so long with what they chose,
You almost missed what you needed most.
All your days were stuck in a rhythm
That you couldn't change or stop,
Nothing to say 'cause your words and emotions
Were twisted and chained in a knot.

But I know what you need,
I strum against your strings
And make you sing,
Sing lucky, lucky me,
Sing lucky, lucky me.

The sound travels through her and strikes against the strings of her soul. Deep inside, she begins to feel the vibration. It has rippled all the way to the bottom of the lake through the dark green water.

She sees the boat, far above her, on the surface. Tripp is playing the guitar. They are singing. The day is beautiful.

She tries to rise toward the boat, but the weight of the water is too heavy. And then she hears his voice. . . .

We can't let this pass us by,
Can't let it go without a fight.
We are who we're meant to be,
Singing lucky, lucky me.

TRIPP'S ROOM; 11:31 P.M.

Tripp is lying in his bed, unable to sleep, when his phone buzzes. He answers.

"Is this Tripp? This is Lyla's dad."

Tripp sits up. "Yeah, it's me."

"Sorry for calling so late, but . . ." Tripp hears Mr. Marks choke back tears, and he feels as if his heart has stopped beating. "She . . . she squeezed my hand." Tripp hears his happy laugh break through. "It's a really good sign. It's what we've been waiting for, Tripp."

A chill runs up Tripp's spine.

"I'll call you tomorrow and give you a progress report."

"Thanks," Tripp says.

There is a moment of silence on the other end and then Mr. Marks says, "I think it was the music, Tripp. Your music."

The tears stream down Tripp's face and he breaks into a smile. When the call is over, he gets out of bed and knocks on his mom's door.

"Tripp? What is it?"

He opens it, and she sits up in bed and switches on her light.

He looks at her, happy that she is here, in her plain nightgown and her messed-up hair with that worried look on her face, to witness what he is about to say.

"Lyla's dad called." He smiles. "She squeezed his hand."

DECEMBER–MARCH

To: gillias_t@crenshaw.com
From: tBroody@broodyrc.com
Date: 12-1
Re: Tripp Broody

Dear Mr. Gillias,

My son and I have discussed it and have decided that it is best for him to remain in his current school. We enjoyed meeting the Crenshaw staff and thank you for your time.

M+H METRO HEALTHCARE, LLC.

To: Franklin Marks
From: Husna Ahuja, M.D.

Dear Mr. Marks,

Great news. Results from the neurological tests came back yesterday. No residual problems with brain or motor functioning. Everything looks normal. Report from Point Orthopedics indicates that Lyla responded well to physical therapy and the follow-up x-ray of the femur was also normal. She should be able to participate fully in school and continue with extracurricular activities. We'd like to see her for a follow-up in two weeks.

Name: *Tripp Broody*

Physics Unit Exam

Perfect!

1. When a sound source approaches you, the pitch you hear is

a. lower than when the source is stationary

(b.) higher than when the source is stationary

c. the same as when the source is stationary

d. first higher and then lower than the pitch of the source when stationary

2. To calculate the frequency of an electromagnetic wave, you need to know the speed of the wave and its

(a.) wavelength

b. refraction

c. intensity

d. amplitude

3. Electromagnetic waves vary in

a. the speed they travel in a vacuum

(b.) wavelength and frequency

c. the way they reflect

d. the orientation of their electric and magnetic fields

A note from Annie...

Hey Lyla,

I'm glad we talked it all out, too. I decided to say yes to Coles after all. I'm excited & scared. I'll probably hate it, but I agree with my mom that it's too important to not try.

I found out that Bethany, that girl we met at camp last year, is going so I'll at least know one other person. I'll miss you & everybody at Rockland, except for a few people & teachers. Ha ha. BTW I listened to your songs on your website, & I thought they were amazing. Really.

Love, Annie

<To: Lyla Marks> February 16

Lyla, I was just listening to our recording of Lucky Me. You should add cello! I could hear it in my head and it sounded so cool.

House of
Musical Traditions

Date: 03/10   Time: 4:07
Staff: Molly   Trans: 4628823

COPY

Luna Acoustic Guitar $399.00

SUBTOTAL   399.00
SALES TAX   24.94
TOTAL   423.94

THANK YOU FOR SHOPPING WITH US!

MARCH 28. SATURDAY.

TRIPP'S ROOM; 10:01 A.M.

. . . SUNNY AND WARM. HIGHS AROUND 50. SOUTHWEST WINDS FIVE TO TEN MILES PER HOUR. 97.3 FM WEATHER. STAY TUNED TO THIRTY MINUTES OF UNINTERRUPTED MUSIC BROUGHT TO YOU BY . . .

The sound of the radio drills into Tripp Broody's ears, and his eyelids open. His right hand reaches up and swats off the clock's alarm button. Why is his alarm on? It's Saturday. After three slow blinks, he notices the note stuck between the strings of his guitar, which is in the stand by his bed.

Dear Tripp,

Before I went to work this morning, Lyla's dad called asking if he and Lyla could swing by and pick you up at 10:30. So I set your alarm. I'll let them explain what it's about. It's fine with me if you want to do it. Have a great day, and tell me all about it when I come home.

Love, Mom

Tripp lifts up the shade of his window. The sky is cloudless; the trees are all green with new leaves. His phone buzzes. A message from Lyla.

Lyla/are you up?
Tripp/yeah. what's going on?
Lyla/not telling. we'll be there soon. bye.

He pulls on jeans and a shirt and eats a quick breakfast. After a few minutes, there is a knock on the door, and Tripp runs to answer it.

Lyla is standing on his steps in her red coat, with her black beret over her short hair, a guitar case in her hand.

"Hello, Mr. Odd," she says, smiling.

"Hello, Ms. Even," he says.

"Get your guitar because . . ." She grins.

"What?"

"We have a gig today," she says.

"We do?"

271

She pulls a piece of paper from her pocket and hands it to him.

Washington Metropolitan Transit Authority
Musicians in the Metro Permit
Granted to Tripp Broody and Lyla Marks

Behind her, waiting, is her dad in his car.

"Are you in?" she asks.

He smiles. "Indeed."

When they arrive at the station, Tripp and Lyla show their permit to the Metro attendant and set up on the platform. People are streaming off the train and through the Metro turnstile: business types in suits, shoppers with bags, everybody in a hurry.

Even though they have a permit, they still feel self-conscious in the bustling, focused atmosphere. People are here to get on and off trains, not to hear music. But Tripp and Lyla tune up and look at each other for encouragement, and when they start to play, the chords rise and echo off the curved walls with such a bright, huge sound, there is no turning back.

They begin to sing. Tripp relaxes into the sound and lets his voice pour out. Lyla feels his confidence and sings out, too.

A woman pulling a wheeled suitcase steps off the train, and when she hears the music, she stops and listens. The trains whoosh by. A man carrying a small boy stops. He sets down his son and listens with him, nodding his head. The boy bends his knees up and down to the beat, and the dad grins.

Tripp and Lyla sing, and their song rides on a wave in all directions: it fills the station, and enters into the ears of all the people getting off the trains, and rises up the long escalators, and flows out into the March air.

And they are thrumming.

THE THRUM SOCIETY SONGBOOK

Words and Music by
Tripp Broody and Lyla Marks

WWW.THRUMSOCIETY.COM

A Little Room to Play

VERSE

G
Fill in the blank, it's time for a test
G
As soon as I'm done, it's on to the next
C   G
True or false, just choose the one that's best
A7   Am7   D   Dsus4
Through the halls, I'm running out of breath

CHORUS

  C   Dadd4   C   G
But now I've got myself a little room to play
  C   Dadd4   C   Dadd4
Now I've got myself a little room to play
  C   Dadd4   Em   Dadd4   C   G
All my worries fade away . . .   as soon as I start to play

VERSE

G
Someone measures every step of mine
G
A to B straight down the line

```
C                           G
Everybody's waiting all the while
A7                  Am7          D  Dsus4
I'm supposed to show up and smile
```

REPEAT CHORUS

BRIDGE

```
D               F/D        D         F/D
Now no one's watching me . . . No one hears
D      F/D                   C        Dsus4
I walk into the room ... And I disappear
```

VERSE

```
G
Why do I choose this way to follow?
G
All the answers are due tomorrow
C                           G
Everybody's waiting all the while
A7                            D  Dsus4
Maybe I won't show up and smile . . . Oh
```

END CHORUS

     C   **Dadd4**   **C**   **G**
'Cause I got myself a little room to play
C   **Dadd4**   **C**   **Dadd4**
Now I've got myself a little room to play
C   **Dadd4**   **Fadd2**   **G***
All my worries fade away… they fade away
Dadd4   **C**   **G**
As soon as I start to play

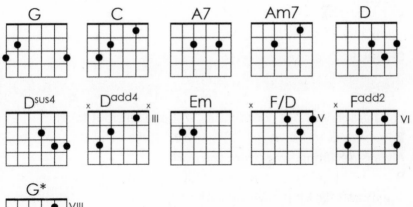

Mr. Odd

VERSE

<pre>
B   A   F#   A
Woke up today, saw my face in the mirror
B   A   F#   A
Eyes don't lie, message is clear
        B   A   F#   A
I can hear it. I can see it. I can say it.
      A#   A
I'm odd.
</pre>

CHORUS

<pre>
          B   A   B   A
I'm a graph without coordinates, a shape without form
B   G   A   A#
Always deviating away from the norm
B   A   B   A
Logic can't fix what's wrong with me
      G   A   B A B A
I'm odd. I'm odd. I'm odd . . .
B A B A
Indeed.
</pre>

VERSE

        B   A F#   A
I've got superhuman cilia in my ear
    B   A   F#   A
Which gives me the ability to hear the fears
     B   A   F#   A
And the lies that people hide behind and what's more
   A#   A
I can hear which crayon's happy in a box of sixty-four

REPEAT CHORUS

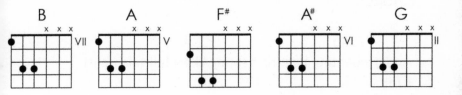

281

Tell-Tale Heart

VERSE

E7   **A7**
Guilt on my sleeve and the bottom of my shoe
E7   **A7**
Guilt under my collar, sticks to me like glue
E7   **A7**
Swallowed it on Sunday, and it's eatin' me alive
B7   **A7**
Buried it on Monday, but it just won't die

CHORUS

     E7#9   **A7***
And it's beating beating beating like a tell-tale heart
E7#9   **A7***
Beating beating beating like a tell-tale heart
E7#9   **A7***
Beating beating beating like a tell-tale heart
B7*   **A7***   **B7**
Can't make it stop once it starts

VERSE

E7   **A7**
Guilt on my tongue leaves a bitter taste

```
E7                          A7
```
Guilt in my bloodstream, running through my veins
```
E7                          A7
```
Hide it on Tuesday, but I got no choice
```
B7                          A7
```
Friday rolls around, and you can hear it in my voice 'cause it's

REPEAT CHORUS

BRIDGE

```
A7*                              B7*
```
Don't tell me you can't hear it when I walk into the room

```
A7*                          B7*
```
Louder every minute, going boom boom boom

REPEAT CHORUS

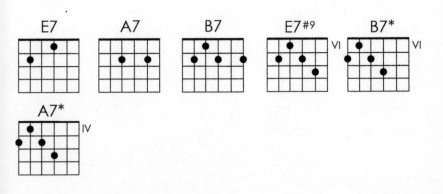

Guilty

VERSE

E7
Cheatin, lying, and conniving
A7
Fraud and forgery
E7
Aggravated screaming
      A7
Dreaming of conspiracy
E7
Flawed in every thought
      A7
I'm a twisted guarantee
      B7
I'm a menace I'm a thorn
      A7
I should never have been born

CHORUS

    E7   **A7**
I'm guilty oh guilty (x3)
     B7   **A7**
Doin' time for my crime

VERSE

E7
War crimes
     A7
Won't deny 'em
E7
Busted, tried
     A7
Without a trial
E7
No lawyer by my side
    A7
I'm just hanging out to dry
    B7
I'm a menace I'm a thorn
    A7
I should never have been born

REPEAT CHORUS

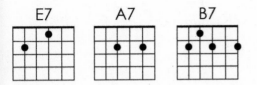

The Pomegranate Waltz

VERSE

C   Esus4   Am G
I like the sound of your name in my ear
C   Esus4   Dm7 G
I like to hear what you have to say
          C   Esus4
I'd like to pay attention to you—
Dm7   G
Instead of doing what I have to do
  D7sus4   G
Oh . . .

CHORUS

C   Am
Now something inside me is ready
C   Am
Something inside me is ready
D7sus4   Fm
Something in me's ready—oh—here I go . . .

VERSE

C   Esus4   Am G
I like the way that our time intertwines
          C   Esus4   Dm7 G
I want to design each day so we can meet

                C   **Esus4** **Dm7**
Each word a seed that's hoping to grow—no need to hurry.
G
Let's take it slow
  D7sus4   **G**
Oh...

REPEAT CHORUS

VERSE

C   **Esus4**   **Am** **G**
I like the shape of the thoughts in your mind
           C   **Esus4**   **Dm7** **G**
You've got the kind of edge that I seem to need
        C   **Esus4** **Dm7**
And if you feel the world doesn't care—I'll send a message.
G   **D7sus4** **G**
You'll know I'm here. Oh . . .

CHORUS (repeat last line and end on C)

Waiting in a Tree

VERSE

        A   G   A   G
I'm gonna wait out on this limb
        A   G   A   G
All by myself and count my sins
        A   G   A   G
While ants go marching two by two
        A   G   A   G
Looking for you

CHORUS

A   G   C
Hang on . . . Hang on . . . Waiting for somebody to come
A   G   E
Hang on . . . Hang on . . . Rescue me from what I have done

VERSE

        A   G   A   G
I should go cause you are late
        A   G   A   G
stuck with the hook, forgot the bait
         A   G   A   G
The seconds crawl, the minutes stall

```
      A          G      A      G
I'm gonna fall
```

REPEAT CHORUS

```
     A          G           A      G
Rock paper scissors and the paper covers rock
           A          G           A      G
I can't even win against myself, I'm all out of luck
     A          G           A      G
Rock paper scissors and the paper flies away
           A      G      A      G
Saying: I don't got all day
```

REPEAT CHORUS

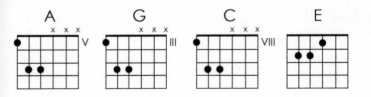

Get Away

VERSE

```
        D              A
I'll be Bonnie; you be Clyde
        D              A
Steal the snow out of the sky
        D          Bm      G   A
Steal a joke and let it fly . . . let it fly
          D            A
Steal the show with your disguise
        D            A
Hide away from prying eyes
          D          Bm          G
Steal the fun and say surprise . . . say surprise
```

PRE-CHORUS

```
Em              G   A
I got to get away somehow
Em              G   A
I got to get away right now
```

CHORUS

```
D                     A                    Em
Got to get away Got to get away Got to get away
```

```
G                      A
Come on, baby, we can't be late
G                          A
Got a little something to celebrate
D                      A                    Em
Got to get away Got to get away Got to get away
G      A      D
Got to get away
```

VERSE

```
      D              A
Keep on running til the dawn
      D              A
No more tired in your yawn
    D            Bm              G      A
Grab the going from your gone . . . Til it's gone, gone, gone
      D          A
Steal the lulla from your bye
      D          A
No more longing in your sigh
      D            Bm            G
Steal the wrong and make it right . . . make it right
```

REPEAT PRE-CHORUS

REPEAT CHORUS

BRIDGE

```
Em                G   A
                 Oh...
Em                G   A              B
I got to get away right now, right now...
E                        B
Run away, ride away (Got to get away)
E                         B
Steal away in style away (Got to get away)
E                         B
Me away a mile away (Got to get away)
E             B
Do it all my a-way (Got to get away)
A             B
We got to fly today
A             B
Skid on the sky today
```

REPEAT CHORUS TWICE IN NEW KEY

```
E                        B                   F#m
Got to get away Got to get away Got to get away
A                 B
Come on, baby, we can't be late
A                      B
Got a little something to celebrate
E                        B                   F#m
Got to get away Got to get away Got to get away
```

A   B   E

Got to get away

A   B   E

Got to get away

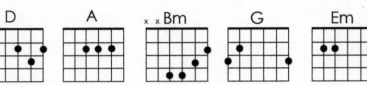

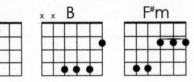

D   A   x x Bm   G   Em

E   x x B   F#m

Lucky Me

VERSE

Em   **D6/F#**
The sun was tied up in clouds and
      G   **D6/F#**
The moon wrung out of its songs
Em   **D6/F#**
Up on 12th Street the trees were just trees,
        G   **D6/F#**
Holding nothing but leaves in their arms
       Em   **D6/F#**
All my days were locked in a closet
      G   **D6/F#**
With the rags and the brooms and the mops
        Em   **D6/F#**
Nothing to feel but the feel of nothing
      G   **D6/F#**
Slipping through keyholes and locks

CHORUS

     Em   **Em7**
But you know what I need
     A   **Am**
You strum against my strings and make me
Em   **G**   **D**
Sing . . .

```
     C          G          D
Sing lucky lucky, lucky lucky me
     C          G          D
Sing lucky lucky, lucky lucky me
```

VERSE

```
Em                  D6/F#                      G
You were telling your little white lie making everybody happy,
      D6/F#
Crying inside
Em                  D6/F#
Staying so long with what they chose,
  G                      D6/F#
You almost missed what you needed most
        Em          D6/F#
All your days were stuck in a rhythm
        G                    D6/F#
That you couldn't change or stop
        Em          D6/F#
Nothing to say 'cause your words and emotions
  G                        D6/F#
Were twisted and chained in a knot
```

CHORUS

```
      Em        Em7          A                Am
But I know what you need I strum against your strings
And make you
```

Em   G   D
Sing...

    C   **G**   **D**
Sing lucky lucky, lucky lucky me

    C   **G**   **B7**
Sing lucky lucky, lucky lucky me

BRIDGE

      Em   **D6/F#**   **G**   **D6/F#**
We can't let this pass us by, can't let it go without a fight

     Em   **D6/F#** **G** **D6/F#**
We are who we're meant to be

      Em   **G**   **D**
Singing lucky lucky, lucky lucky me

    C   **G**   **D**
Sing lucky lucky, lucky lucky me (you make me sing)

 C   **G**   **D**
Lucky lucky, lucky lucky me

REPEAT TO END

 Em
 D6/F#
 G
 Em7
 A

 Am
 D
 C
 B7

Acknowledgments

My thanks, first and foremost, go to my editor Regina Griffin for believing in my characters even before they were fully formed. For helpful comments on early drafts, thanks to Karen Giacopuzzi, Lucia Lostumbo, Molly, Michael, and Cissie Williams, my nephew Brian, and my family Max, Simon, and Ivan. Two great books and one awesome CD inspired me along the way: *Zen Guitar* (Simon & Schuster, 1997) by Philip Toshio Sudo; *From Where You Dream: The Process of Writing Fiction* (Grove Press, 2005) by Robert Olen Butler and Janet Burroway; and *Art of Motion* (CandyRat Records, 2005) by Andy McKee. I am grateful to musicians Dede Wyland, Suzanne Brindamour, and Mark Sylvester for feedback on the songs in the book and to Cletus Kennelly at the Urban Garden Recording Studio for making the recording process a joy. A shout-out to Crazy Dave for allowing Lyla to buy her Luna guitar at House of Musical Traditions and my admiration to Yvonne at Luna Guitars for creating such inspiring instruments. Thanks also to Jillian Van Ells, who encouraged me to test-drive the songs, and to the girls at Holton-Arms School and the boys at Landon for being such enthusiastic audiences. Finally, a special thanks to Bill Williams for jumping in to collaborate on Tripp and Lyla's music with such a fun and fearless attitude. Lucky, lucky me.